AN INKED HEARTS NOVEL

Tattooed HEARTS

DARLENE RODRIGUEZ

Tattooed Hearts

Cover Design: Anna Noel

Formatter: Darlene Rodriguez

Editor: Anna Noel

To my TAR syndrome girlies who read books wishing they could see themselves in one, here's a romance staring a main character with Tar Syndrome.

*To everyone who is looking for some kind of validation that you can
be loved despite your disabilities, race, gender, etc.*

Playlist

Tattooed Heart - Ariana Grande
No Judgement - Niall Horan
Moonlight- Ariana Grande
Fictional - Khloe Rose
What Makes You Beautiful - One Direction
Dirty Little Secret - All American Rejects
Bless The Broken Road - RascalFlatts
10,000 Hours - Dan + Shy, Justin Bieber
If I Ever Fall In Love - Shai
Here - Alessia Cara
This is me- Kesha
Flashlight - Jessie J
Little Things - One Direction

AUTHOR'S NOTE

Dear Reader,

Thank you so much for giving this story a try. Tattooed Hearts is at its core a love letter to people like me who struggle to love themselves because of societal norms and found solace in creating a space they could belong to.

When I was growing up there were never any stories about a disabled character who looked like me or had the same disability I had. I was limited on what I could and couldn't do like playing sports, getting a piercing or a tattoo because I also had a bleeding disorder on top of my physical disabilities. Every struggle, every disorder piled up onto one another just made me feel alone—more alone than you could possibly imagine. There was limited access to things like the internet and social media pretty much just starting. In my own little world, there was no one like me. And I felt like this for a long time. Not only was I alone, but I was picked on for being different. I couldn't love myself because how could I when there was nothing around to show me I could be loved?

So I wrote this book, Tattooed Hearts, for those who have TAR syndrome and are looking for some validation that they can be loved. That their disability doesn't define their worth. For others, regardless of their disabilities, race, gender, etc. who weren't shown they could be loved and need to know no matter who they are, they can be loved.

Because you can be loved.

Living with a disability, no matter the severity is tough and each person goes through life differently than the next. Although the main characters in this story are based off of my life experiences and what I've witnessed through my own eyes, they are their own characters with their own thoughts, emotions, and feelings.

Our MMC has a transgender sibling because I feel like a story with a transgender main character is not my story to tell, but I wanted to include this because I have a transgender sibling. And, our FMC is physically disabled because I want to spread awareness about a condition that isn't well known. And if I'm being completely transparent, I wanted to finally be able to see a main character with my disability. You may not relate to her entirely, and that's okay.

There will be moments of transphobia and discrimination against people who are transgender and physically disabled from a side character in this book, however, I do not condone these beliefs.

This is not the theme of this story, but I wanted to put it out there because I understand stories and scenes can be harmful to communities.

*** *If either of these topics isn't in your favor, please do not continue to read. I do not condone hate or bullying and would rather you see yourself out here and now. But if you'd like to keep reading, please continue with an open heart and mind.*

Tattooed Hearts is a story that's dear to my heart for so many reasons and I hope you love these characters as much as I do.

Thank you for your patience with me.

If you are reading or downloaded this book from a pirating site, it is stolen and posted without my permission.
Please be aware this puts you at risk of a malware attack.

CONTENT WARNING

discrimination
depression
anxiety
flashback of attempted suicide by a sibling (in chapter 33),
Transphobia by a side character

***If these trigger you in any way, please do not harm yourself by continuing to read. I rather you take care of yourself than read something that will bring up bad memories.

"Moonlight"

PROLOGUE

CASSIUS

SIX MONTHS AGO

The smell of lavender seeps into the atmosphere as an angel appears at my tattoo station.

My heart thumps in my throat. She's dressed in a pink, blue, and white knit sweater, her sleeves rolled up, revealing her arms. They aren't like mine... they're shorter. Like she doesn't have a forearm. I've never seen anyone like that before. I shouldn't be staring, but my gaze continues to wander over her—not missing her plump rosy lips or those bright silver eyes that call out to me like the moon.

She's gorgeous, but with the way she bows her head and tries to hide her arms, it's clear she doesn't think the same.

"How can I help you?" I ask. Nerves creep up the back of my neck and my throat constricts. I lift the water bottle in my hand to my lips and take a sip, needing something to ease my thirst.

"They said you're the guy I should see to help with my virginity."

I choke at her words, inhaling the water into my lungs. I cough for relief, trying my best to clear the liquid from my airways. She's the first woman to catch me off guard, not the first to nearly kill me, though.

"I'm sorry, I didn't mean to make you choke. Usually, I'm the one choking." Her wide silver eyes latch onto me as her hands fly to her mouth.

A smirk curls onto my lips even as I continue to keep myself from dying from the water I accidentally inhaled.

"No, it's fine," I manage to let out. "I don't mind getting choked."

And now it's my turn to mentally face-palm. I clear my throat and shake my head. Changing the subject sounds like the best option. "So which do you want?"

"Huh?" She tilts her head.

"Do you want to be marked or pierced?" I explain. Cece, my sister, and front desk attendant, laughs her ass off outside my office. I walk over to the woman, hold my hand out over her shoulder, and close the door for privacy. "I can do whichever you'd like."

My gaze drops to her. She's looking up at me with those beautiful moonlight eyes. I'm stuck on them, hypnotized. The overpowering scent of her—lavender—makes me lightheaded. It's too much—intoxicating. I can barely focus. And the moment her pouty rosy lips part, my heart skips a beat.

I'm in trouble.

"Tattoo," she whispers. "I want them to see beauty when they stare at my arms."

I furrow my eyebrows, lowering my attention to her arms. She holds them out and I take a step back, reaching for her but stop as I look up at her. "Can I?"

She nods her head, giving me permission. I gently take her

left elbow in my hand. My fingers run over the soft *S-shaped* scar running down from the end of her thumb, over her wrist, and to her elbow.

"I was born with a missing bone," she explains, not clarifying which. Not that it matters. I can clearly see it's the one between her elbow and wrist.

I let go of her left arm and take the other. It's different, more bent at the elbow than her left. This scar looks like the number four, but it's connected to another one, making it look like a ship. It curves into a *C* and the end runs higher. My thumb follows it, lifting her sleeve until it reaches just below her shoulder. Her arm is thin like it might be all bone. I can easily wrap my entire hand around it. Both scars are surgical and they look like they've been there for years. I don't press on them. I'm not sure if it'd cause her any discomfort or pain if I did.

Why did they do this to her?

"And this one?" I ask, voice barely above a whisper.

"A surgery gone wrong…"

But what were they trying to do? And why not make sure they could do it before fucking it up?

"How old were you?"

"I was a baby for most of them, the last one I was ten and I didn't want them to keep trying to make me normal."

Not her arms. Her.

I swallow the thought. The more my gaze lingers on her scars, the more my blood boils—angry that the world made her believe something was wrong with *her*. But I understand. Not everyone is comfortable or likes the body they were born into.

I take a step back before her scent traps me again. "It's gonna be kind of hard to ink over what's already beautiful if you ask me," I tell her. "Your scars show strength."

"They show deformity and make people stare like I'm some circus freak."

My lips press into a thin line. I won't argue with the perception she has of herself. Not when I don't even know her name. "Alright. So what would you like?"

"Something to cover the scars."

Lucky for her, they are old enough to work over. The problem is mainly where they're located. Even a mature scar can be sensitive, especially surgical ones.

Besides, tattoo or not, it won't change the fact that she has small arms—people will still stare—and it also won't change the way she feels about herself, only she can do that. However, I don't tell her either of those things. I'm sure she knows. Part of me wants to snap on a pair of gloves, assess the scars with my fingers, and see just how tough they would be. But the other part of me knows something like this will take some time, even if I make sure it'll be okay.

"I'll think about it," I tell her.

Her eyebrows draw together. "What do you mean, *you'll think about it?*"

"It's going to be a big tattoo and I don't want you to regret it down the line," I say, shrugging my shoulders, "and most people regret their first one."

"Now you sound like my dad." She crosses her arms, not liking my answer. "I make my own decisions."

A chuckle leaves my lips. Clearly, she's able to because if she couldn't, she wouldn't be here, in my shop. "I'll make you a deal."

I raise my hands over my head, interlocking my fingers. Normally, I don't question anyone's decisions, but on rare occasions—different from the one I'm in now—I give my customers the option.

"I'll give you a tattoo today," I tell her, not wanting to take away her independence. "Something small of your choice. And if you can last two months without wanting to get rid of it, we can start working on the one you want."

"What makes you think I won't just go elsewhere?"

"Simple." I meet her gaze. There's a fire in her eyes, one I can't help but admire. "I can take care of you better than anyone else can."

She stills. Heat rushes to her face, tinting those pretty round cheeks. "You don't even know me."

"No, but I know myself." I hold her gaze. "And I'm very confident in my skills."

Her lips part but then close. Her eyebrows draw together before she speaks. "Do you have anything with letters or a typewriter?"

A smile rises to my lips. "I might, we can check together."

Moving to the side, I hold my arm out, silently encouraging her to take a seat on the tattoo bed. My station is small, much like everyone else's in this shop, but at least it gives our customers—and my employees—privacy. My walls are plain, freshly painted black, with no art or decorations. That'll change once I get some extra money for art supplies.

She passes by me and her lavender scent pulls me in again. She's exhilarating, and I don't even know her but I plan to— for work purposes, that is.

And an hour is more than enough time to do just that.

"Before we get started, did Cece have you fill out a form?" I ask.

She takes a seat and nods. Her eyes are on the floor as she swings her legs off the side of the tattoo bed. "I just didn't give it back to her. I had a few questions she said you could answer."

"Alright." I walk over to my desk—a mess of ink tubes and papers. It usually is on busy days like today has been, but once it's over, my desk will be cleared and clean. I pull out my stool, sit down, and wheel it over by the bed.

"Go on," I encourage.

She lowers her head, eyes on her hands as they fiddle in her lap. "Well, on the form it asks about difficulty to stop the bleeding."

"We ask because it will puncture your skin. We don't want anyone to risk bleeding for long periods. It's a safety precaution. It can affect the healing process and make it a little difficult. But that doesn't prevent you from getting the tattoo. You just have to take it into consideration."

She hums and I'm not sure why, but I have to ask, "Does your blood have a hard time clotting?"

Her fingers curl around the ends of her sweater as she nods.

"That does complicate things," I tell her and sigh. "However, you look like a smart woman, and I wouldn't want to say no without you asking your doctors first. So how about I give you a temporary tattoo? It'll wear off in about a week. It gives you enough time to check in with them. This way if they say it should be fine, you can give the shop a call and I'll schedule you in."

She looks up at me. Her silver eyes are like rain clouds, ready to burst with tears. A sharp pain tugs at my chest. I don't even know this woman and I already can't stand the tears bubbling in her eyes.

"I'm not keeping you from making a decision," I tell her.

My hand reaches out and lands on hers. "You can even call today and run back here the moment they say yes."

"Really?" She sniffles, her nose turning a shade of pink. "You mean it?"

The corner of my lips tugs upward into a smile and I give her hand a gentle squeeze. "Of course."

The moment she blinks, a lone tear trails down her face. My hand moves on its own, cupping her cheek as my finger brushes her tear away. My gaze drifts back up to her wide eyes. A blush spreads across her cheeks, my heart hammering at the sight.

Maybe I shouldn't have done that.

But before I can open my mouth to apologize, her lips brush gently across mine. They barely touch, and yet it's like she's taken all the air from my lungs. Everything else around us seems to fade away: the buzzing sounds from the other rooms, the black walls, and my entire station. There's nothing except for me and her... in this time and space.

I don't even know who she is, let alone her name and she's caught me off guard twice in less than an hour.

Her eyes are shut as she lingers, almost as if she's waiting for me to push her away or stop her. I don't, but there's a small voice that reels its way to the front of my mind.

"It's me or this place. It can't be both."

I swallow down the ultimatum given to me nearly a year ago. I promised I'd never put myself back in a position like that. And if I didn't stop now, it wouldn't be fair to either of us.

My hand slips from her cheek and drops to her shoulder, gently guiding her away. "I'm sorry, I just..."

A sudden knock at the door brings us both back to reality. The black walls of my station surround us. The hum of an ink gun fills the background noise, and her lavender smell drifts further away.

And the realization I almost kissed a client punches me right in the gut.

My feet kick against the floor, pushing more distance between me and the woman on my tattoo bed. I clear my throat and spin around on the stool just in time for the door to open.

"There's an asshole on the phone demanding to talk to you," my sister says. Cece never disturbs me when I have a client, which means it's serious. She crosses her arms over her chest, and her eyes dart between me and the woman. "Should I just hang up on them?"

I sigh, shaking my head. "No. It's fine. I'll be right out."

My sister nods and closes the door, leaving me alone once more. I turn to the woman. Her gaze focuses on her hands as her pointer fingers tap together.

My lip twitches. *She's so fucking cute.*

"I should go," she says, hopping down from the tattoo bed. "Thank you for the consideration and I'm sorry... for kissing you."

She doesn't look at me, too focused on leaving in a hurry. My fingers long to reach out, pull her back, and explain everything. But I don't.

Her hand wraps around the doorknob as she glances back at me. Those moonlight eyes swirl with questions she wants to ask and I'm drawn in, ready to answer whatever they might be. Instead, she gives me the sweetest goodbye I've ever heard. "Bye, Sunlight."

I blink twice and heat flushes right to my cheeks.

Sunlight... why would she—

The reasoning clicks instantly. My eyes shift to various

shades of brown, mostly when the sun or light hits them, but sometimes, they just shift… like it tries to match my mood or something.

None of that matters to me though. She has one foot out the door and I still don't know what her name is, though there's one thing I'll definitely remember her by.

But she's gone before I can say anything.

I sigh, letting my words drift in the space between us. "Goodbye, *Moonlight*."

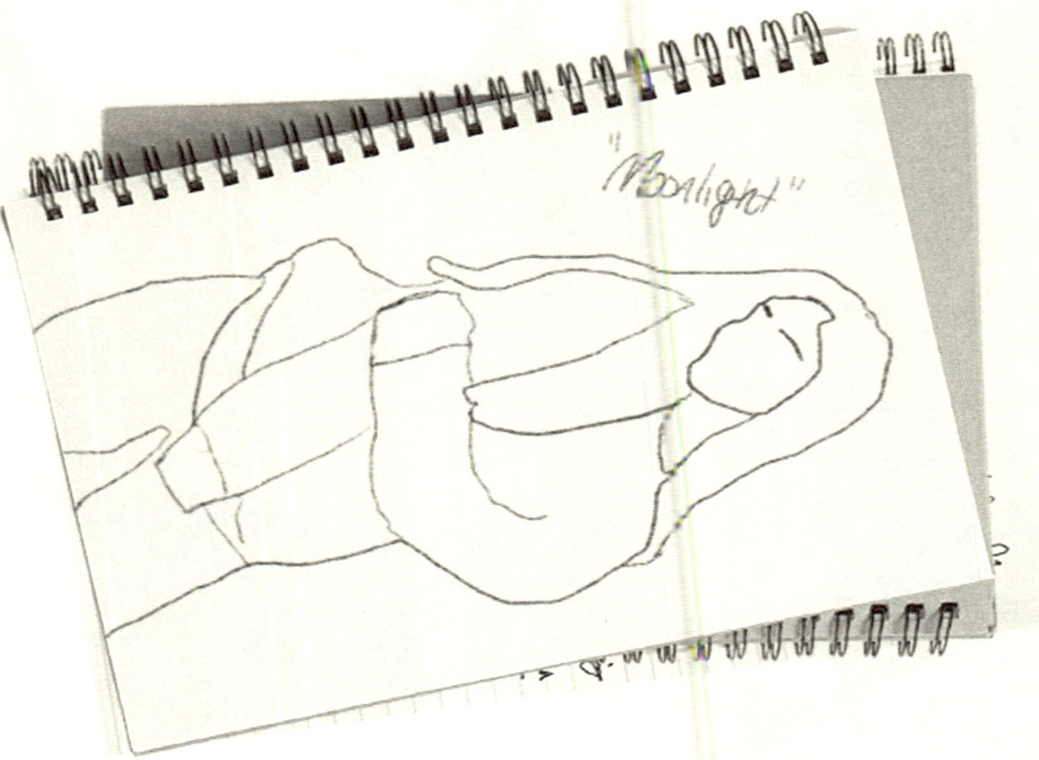

"Moonlight"

1

RESPECT GOES A LONG WAY

CASSIUS

PRESENT

Roommate wanted, and possibly a new best friend. My best friend moved in with her ~~dog~~ boyfriend off campus, leaving me friendless. Text me if interested. LGBTQIA+ or allies only.

I read over the flyer stacked on top of the others in my hands. Chatter echoes around the dining hall I'm standing in, but nothing really stands out except for the smell of marinara sauce and Italian spices filling the air.

I want to leave, but I can't. Not until I'm done.

"Don't you think this is a little over the top?" I ask, turning to my sister as she tapes one of her flyers up onto a corkboard.

Her brown curls bounce as she turns to me and her painted blue lips twist into a smile. Her eyebrows raise like I should know better than to ask such a question. "I could have written worse, Cass."

That she could have. Cece is the definition of over the top.

She's extreme, demanding, and not afraid to be herself. She might be my little sister, but I admire the living shit out of her.

"But for Xyli's sake, I chose not to. She's my best friend after all." She shrugs. "And one day she'll be Mave's future."

I chuckle and shake my head. "You know he'd kill you if you tell him that."

"Oh, I know." I listen to her as I grab a paper from the stack in my hand, place it on the corkboard, and let Cece tape it down. "With that deathly glare of his. But other than that, he's a little softy."

Our cousin, Maverick—or Mave as we call him—definitely is a quiet, broody shit with a soft heart. I don't know all the details about Xyli and to be honest, I don't care for them. Cece, on the other hand, loves to know everything and anything she can, so I always hear about it second-hand.

"Too bad she's with his best friend," I add so she doesn't think I'm not listening.

"Oh, I'm not too concerned about that." She grins and I worry she has something up her sleeve. "Things will play out the way they need. She'll see he's not worth it and Mave will come to her rescue."

Did Xyli really need that though? Granted, I don't know the girl on a personal level. *Maybe she did...* I shrug the thought away and get back to more important things.

"And the other part of the flyer, what's that about?" I ask.

Cece rolls her eyes, taping another flyer down. "My roommate was one of those stuffy people who hate the LGBTQIA+ community. I know not all people are like that. I even respected her beliefs but she couldn't respect me so she found a new dorm."

And with that, Cece doesn't go on. She doesn't need to. I understand, but there's still an ache gnawing in my chest.

People can be cruel to what they don't understand—what they chose not to understand in some instances. It isn't fair and I hate that my sister has to go through these kinds of troubles on a daily basis. She's a person with a good heart and that should be enough for the world.

"Here," she pulls me from the bitter feeling, splitting the stack of flyers in my hand before holding her half close to her chest. "We'll cover more ground this way."

With that, Cece heads left and I go right. The chatter from the noisy dining hall finally set in, crowding my mind before the little worries, like someone knocking her down or tossing her flyers, begin to make their way to the front.

I shake my head. *I have a job to do. For her.*

Leaving the dining hall, I tape the flyers everywhere I can. From pillars to bulletin boards, and even building doors. I place the flyers anywhere people can spot them. My sister deserves to have a roommate if that's what she wants and with luck, it will be someone nice.

I can only hope for that.

Luckily, it's a nice day out. The temperature may have dropped to sixty degrees Fahrenheit, but the autumn breeze barely blows by, allowing the surrounding trees to keep their eye-catching red and yellow leaves.

My hoodie might stop the cold from getting in, but not from it nipping at my fingertips. It's almost like autumn is trying to hold hands.

"You're defacing school property." A voice I loath hearing calls. Chancellor James Watson.

I turn to the side, away from the brick building of our

campus library, glancing over his figure. He stands tall, head held high and his tie neatly pressed to his shirt. We hardly cross paths anymore. In fact, I moved off campus because of him.

If it weren't for my siblings enrolling at the school, I would have been long gone. But they're here and I'm in my last year of classes, living alone, while they live the college experience in the dorms because they want to. And who am I to deny them their choice?

"If it were my own flyers, I'd consider that statement, but it's not. I'm helping my sister put them up."

Watson narrows his steel-blue eyes at me and looks over the flyers. He raises an eyebrow before his gaze darts back to me. "*He* shouldn't be looking for a roommate. In fact, *he* shouldn't be allowed to live on campus."

The man wracks my every nerve. He pokes my patience each time he refers to my sister as *he*. Cece isn't a male. In fact, Cece has always just been Cece to me. And the moment she came out to me, I accepted who she was. Not everyone was as accepting though. It took my brother a while to call Cece by her pronouns and even now, he slips up. But the Chancellor does it with purpose and intent.

Respect goes a long way, especially with me, and the Chancellor doesn't have mine. Not when he blatantly has none for me or my sister. "She has every right just as much as the other students."

I don't understand why he has authority. People as disrespectful as him shouldn't have as much power as he does. But that's life, right? Unfair and unpredictable.

I stand toe to toe with the Chancellor. He glares at me with disgust while I stand up for what's right. Some students around the area stop. I feel their eyes on us and I'm sure he does too.

He scoffs, backing down and stepping away. "As you were Mr. Valencia."

I glare in his direction until he rounds the building and disappears. I wish I could be as I was. Everything was fine until he came to campus during my second year.

The Chancellor never gave me a chance. He took one look at me—my tattoos—and deemed me unworthy just like everyone else who has their head so far up their asses.

But that's fine… they can see me as such. The people I care about know who I am. And that is all that matters.

I ignore the anger itching under my skin and finish putting up the flyers. I don't meet back up with Cece. There's no need, she knows I won't ever let her down.

Moving away from the building, I step onto the quad. The chatter around me becomes background noise the moment I sit on the grass. Colorful leaves surround the area, some blowing past with the wind.

I slide my backpack from my shoulders and place it in front of me. My gaze drifts over the other students as I pull a pencil and my sketchbook out. Flipping through the pages, I stop when I notice the typewriter shaded in with letters flying out. I'd been at this sketch for six months, trying to perfect it just in case a previous client of mine came back.

She said she wanted one, so I planned on showing her some ideas I had specifically for her.

My moonlight.

I lick my lips as the memory draws me back to the day I laid eyes on her bright silver eyes and those pouty pink lips I had the pleasure of tasting.

Even now I can feel her gaze on me. I shake my head and glance up from my sketchbook, catching someone staring in my direction.

I blink, squinting—trying to get a better view of this woman. She's dressed in a pair of black leggings, Doc Martens, and a beige Redwood University hoodie. Her hair is tied in two low pigtails hanging down either side of her shoulders and the top of her head is covered by a black poof ball hat.

My mouth curls into a smile. And like I do with everyone who stares, I start to wave. But the moment I notice the man standing behind her—The Chancellor—I stop and my smile drops. He pulls her in the opposite direction.

I wonder who she is.

Shaking the thought, I don't let it bug me. There are other things to worry about. Like taking care of the bills for Inked Hearts, the tattoo shop I own, preparing for karaoke night at Redwood Tavern where I work part-time on the weekends, providing for my siblings, and most importantly, finishing this project.

Especially this project... for *her*.

2

A GLASS DOLL

MELODY

My steps fall in line with my dad's. He has his hands behind his back—his blue suit buttoned up, and his tie hangs over the blazer. My dad continues to talk about the great opportunities Redwood University will give me now that I've finally *come to terms with my future,* as he puts it, but I'm barely listening. I am already here and enrolled. I let him go on, though, it's best to let him wear himself out.

My gaze drifts over the warm colors of autumn hanging from trees around the quad. The sharp scent of freshly brewed coffee tickles my nose as some students pass by with cups in hand. Others sit on the freshly cut grass occupied with books and notes, while a few rush to class with the same items in their hands, and then there is another.

He's deep into his work, whatever it may be. Ink covers his arms, but I can barely make out the images from the distance separating us. As if he feels someone looking, he glances in my direction. He blinks, squinting to get a better look, and then his lips curl into the most inviting smile I've ever seen in my life.

Ok, that's a lie. I've seen one almost as inviting, but my brain isn't allowing me to pinpoint who or when it might have been.

Still, my heart skips a beat because, for the first time in a while, someone's eyes are on my face rather than the stupid scars on my arms. However, it fades the moment his attention is taken away by something beside me. My dad, no doubt.

A strong hand falls onto my shoulder and I look over to my dad as he pulls me in the opposite direction of the man. I take a quick look behind. He's still staring, watching me. He looks down at his notebook, turns the page, and starts running his pencil over a fresh sheet of paper.

I wonder what he's writing or drawing.

"Melody," my dad says. He clears his throat and I look ahead with a smile.

"Yes?"

"As I was saying, The Dean of Students will make sure to take care of you." He halts in his tracks in front of a brick building. They all pretty much look the same, but I'm assuming it's the student housing building. He turns to me, rubbing both hands over my shoulders; something he used to do to comfort me as a child. I can feel the other students gaze on us, but their footsteps crunch against the grass as they make their way elsewhere.

"I have a meeting to attend, so I'll leave you here."

"Don't worry about me, Dad. I'll be fine."

Worry fills his gaze as they meet mine. He still sees me as his little girl, a porcelain doll, fragile and weak. But I'm not.

He holds his arms out and I sigh, stepping into his

embrace. "I will always worry about you Mel; you're my daughter."

"I know, Dad." I wrap my arms around him, but they don't make it all the way. They never do so I squeeze tight letting him know it's a big hug. His lips press to the top of my head for a second and, then, he pulls away.

"Are you sure you don't want to just move back in with me and your mother? It's not too far."

I shake my head. There's nothing I'd rather do more than avoid living with them at all costs. "No, Dad. I want to live on campus."

He sighs and nods. We've gone over this plenty of times. Luckily, he has a meeting, meaning he won't fight it. "Okay then. Let me know how it goes."

"Of course, I will." I smile up at him, taking a step back. My gaze catches something on the building wall. "What's that?"

My dad turns, his hand pulling a lone flyer from the side of the housing building. He glances over it, body going rigid for a split second before he crumples the paper into a ball. "Nothing important. An old event."

There's more to it, but I don't pester him. As chancellor of the university, he has every right to take down a flyer. I think.

He moves aside and tosses it into the nearest trash bin. Reaching for the door, he opens it for me. I step inside and leave my dad to do whatever he has to do. I look ahead, staring at the long line in front of me—shoulders slumping as a sigh leaves my lips.

I'd been here hours before.

I didn't want to tell my dad I had spoken with housing before meeting up with him. He would have asked me what they said and then forced me into living with him and my mom.

I didn't want that. Not when it meant they'd hover over me and treat me like a child—no, a glass doll.

When I glance over my shoulder, my dad is no longer in sight. *Thank goodness.* I step out of line and head for the door to escape.

My fingers fiddle with one another, gaze scanning around for some alternative. There has to be another option, right? They might not have any dorms or off-campus housing, but they must have something else around, somewhere. I pass the building and head back to the quad. Back at my old school, they had a bulletin board dedicated to rooms on and off campus, and I think I might have seen one around.

My gaze drifts around for the person who caught my eye, but he's nowhere to be found. Instead, I find the bulletin board and head right for it. A flyer written in ocean blue ink catches my attention.

Roommate wanted, and possibly a new best friend.

A chuckle escapes my lips. Already, this person is winning me over with their humor. My eyes continue to scan over the flyer, reading every word.

My best friend moved in with her ~~dog~~ boyfriend off campus, leaving me friendless. Text me if interested. LGBTQIA+ or allies only.

I bounce with excitement. This is my chance. And the last part is a bonus in my opinion. From what I've experienced, those from the LGBTQIA+ community were some of the most welcoming people I've met. They made me feel comfortable like I could be myself. And I'm sure whoever this person is will make me feel the same. I just hope I can show them they'll have a friend in me. Grabbing my phone from my pocket, I text the number on the flyer right away.

Hey, I'm Melody

I saw you were looking for a roommate

I'm interested.

Before I could even shut the screen off, three dots popped up under my message.

UNKNOWN

Are you on campus now?

We can meet up if you're free

I have some time

I lifted my gaze from my phone and glanced around. My dad would be preoccupied for a good while. Worst case, I could tell him they found me one really fast. Though, the flyer never specified a gender... What if they're a guy? Then again, I'd feel just as uncomfortable if it were a girl too. I shake the thoughts from my head. It's my only option at this point. The least I could do is check it out.

Perfect. Where should I meet you?

UNKNOWN

Campbell Hall room 402

I have no idea where that is or if it's even on this campus. *Maybe I could ask for help?* I shake the thought from my head. There are way too many people surrounding the area. Some in groups of two, others much bigger. I can't just go up to them. Not with the itch at the back of my neck intensifying. Not when they'll only see the scars from childhood. Operations decorating my arm. No... I can't.

I'll figure it out on my own.

Spinning on my heels, I head for the nearest map—which is back at the student housing building. I keep my head low, trying not to pay attention to the growing amount of eyes watching me tread through the quad. Being with my dad and walking around was easy because there was a chance they weren't even looking at me, but walking alone... was a different case on its own.

Be brave, be bold, be ballsy.

It's hard when all my insecurities shrivel me up like a leaf in the dead of winter.

Someone bumps into my shoulder, and I stumble. A warm, gentle touch grabs me, keeping me from tumbling back. I catch a whiff of vanilla and sugar and my gaze drifts up. A stubbled beard covers his chin, but not enough to hide his parting lips. Sweet honey brown eyes stare back at me. His hand drops, as does his gaze. My heart beats in my ears, the usual sign that tells me to flee, but I'm rooted to the ground with my mouth agape. And then a soft, kind, and deep voice belts from his.

"Sorry about that."

3

THE SMALLER DETAILS

CASSIUS

There's no response.

The woman I saw with the chancellor a few minutes ago is still staring at me as a blush begins to color her cheeks. She's prettier up close, not that I had any doubts about it. However, I'm not sure how much more I can take with her moonlight eyes pulling me into her orbit. I clear my throat and rub the back of my neck. Leaves crinkle under my shoe as I shift my weight from one foot to the other.

"Are you ok?" I ask, hoping she'll be able to push through her initial shock.

Luckily for me, she nods. Her throat bobs as she swallows. "I-I'm new."

Her voice is sweet, like a tune that can easily implant itself in my brain and get stuck on replay. A small nervous chuckle leaves my lips. "Nice to meet you, I'm Cassius. Cass for short. I hope I didn't scare you."

"No!" She shakes her head. "No, you didn't. I just wasn't expecting to bump into anyone."

"Something to get used to on a big campus," I tell her. My gaze drops and I catch a lump on her right arm surrounded by scars where her sweater sleeves roll up to. Her elbow is slightly bent and turned in. I glance to the left where the soft *S-shaped* scar runs down from the end of her thumb, over her wrist, and down to her elbow.

Holy shit… it is *her*.

"Might as well give them something beautiful to look at while they stare."

That was her excuse when she came to me six months ago, asking me to cover up her scars. And I said I'd think about it.

But she doesn't seem to recognize me.

The fact tugs at my chest more than it should. We shared a kiss and spent one night together. That was all it was meant to be. So why did I want her to remember me?

She moves her arms behind her back and it's only then that I realize I'm staring. I look up at the beauty who still has yet to give me her actual name.

"I was looking for Campbell Hall. Any idea where that might be?" she quickly interjects, averting her gaze from me.

Yeah, I fucked up.

I nod my head anyway and smile. "It's on the south campus by the statue of an old man sitting on a bench and petting a red fox."

She sniffles a laugh, holding her knuckles against her mouth to hide her amusement, not that she needs to. "You mean the one that had a sign saying Old Man Jenkins?"

Cece's doing no doubt.

Every time we passed by that thing, she always greeted the statue as Jenkins. "That's the one. Campbell is the building right there behind it."

"Awesome. Thank you, Cassius."

My name sounds sweet on her tongue and sends a jolt straight through me. I want to hear say it more often.

Her gaze drifts up to my face again and I can't help but smile. She doesn't look at my tattoos, unlike other people. Maybe because she knows what it feels like to be stared at and judged? Or maybe because they don't phase her the same way they had when we first met.

Or it's because most of them are covered by your sweater, idiot.

Still, she doesn't do what I did: stare.

I'm eager to remedy the situation in any way I can. To show her somehow that I wasn't staring in the way she might have thought. The way I might have seemed to be. But first, I needed something from her.

"You're very welcome…" I tilt my head to the side. "New, was it?"

A sweet smile comes to her lips as she shakes her head. "Melody."

The perfect name for a beautiful work of art. "Well, I hope to see you around more often."

She nods in agreement, steps past me, and moves on. I turn, watching her hips move and her brown pigtails bounce against her back. As curious as I still am about her, I can't exactly push myself to go after her. Not when there's a chance it'll scare her off. If she turns back then maybe I can offer to take her, but she doesn't. A sigh leaves my lips as she turns the corner and disappears from my sight.

How did I not realize it was her in the first place? *Maybe because we were outside and not in a stuffy tattoo parlor with dim lights.*

My shoulders slump in disappointment. It's a big school so there's a chance I'll never see her again.

But she might come back for the tattoo. The thought alone fills me with some sense of hope.

Piano notes chime from my phone. Cece's ringtone, Für Elise. I take it out of my pocket and answer.

"Guess what!" she screams from the other end before I even put the phone to my ear.

"What?" I ask, my gaze drifting over the other students walking across the quad with books and a drink in their hands.

"Someone responded to my flyers." I can hear her stomping her feet against the floor, doing her little happy dance no doubt. It's only been two hours since we plastered the flyers on campus so I'm not surprised someone finally messaged her. "I mean it only took a few hours but I'm meeting them here in a few minutes."

A few minutes, alone?

My eyebrows draw together, throat constricting. I know Cece's capable of handling strangers but the big brother in me still worries. "Do you need me to come by?"

"No, Cass. I'll be fine." She waves off, not that it does anything for the nerves crawling under my skin. "Besides, don't you have a class to get to?"

Not necessarily. With running the tattoo shop and managing the bar next door, I haven't had much time for classes. Luckily, I made sure most of them were online. It made it easier for me to hand my work in on time while still doing other things. "No, I'm free right now."

"Oh, so you can take a nap or you know, meet some nice girls for once?"

"You know I don't have time for things like that." I roll my eyes. I tried dating in the past but working, school, owning a tattoo shop, and taking care of my younger siblings left no room for anything else. They are my life. Being a strong support system for them is all I have time for.

"It's just one night."

Melody's words flood back into my brain from six months ago.

Yeah, it was best that it was just that. A moment. Details that seemed so important then, like her physical features, were all pushed to the side because I had other things to take care of. Like making sure my sister would be ok. They seeped through, though.

The smaller details.

The feel of her soft skin under my fingertips. How she smelled like lavender with a hint of vanilla. And the way those pouty lips parted the moment she tilted her head back in ecstasy.

I shake the memories from my head hearing my sister drop something that sounded like a book. "But for you, I'll always have more than enough."

"You need to channel all that love elsewhere." Cece chuckles. "I'm starting to suffocate."

"Yeah, yeah." I wave off, smirking. "Let me know how it goes?"

"Of course. Wouldn't be me if I didn't tell you everything now would I?"

No, she definitely would not.

I debate on telling her about bumping into Melody but decide against it. Knowing Cece she'll do everything in her power to find Melody and drag her into my path every chance she gets. *Not that I'd really complain about that.*

"Make sure to be careful," I remind her.

"Yes, I know." I hear a faint shuffle on the other end of the line before she screeches. I wince at the sudden ringing echoing through my eardrums. "They're downstairs. I gotta go! Love you."

"Love you—" She hangs up before I can finish. I lower the phone from my ear and sigh. "Love you too, sis."

4

WASTSON'S DAUGHTER

MELODY

I should be excited, but fear and anxiety crawl over my skin. I can't do it. There is no way I can push through these doors and meet someone new. Gazes fall over me as I stand here, trying to steady my breath. *Maybe I should just go live with my parents.*

They won't look at me differently. No, but they know.

I'm underdeveloped.

Different.

Deformed.

Each word plays in my mind as I stare at my reflection in the window. The scars of the past adorn my arms, a reminder that not all disappear. Some stay tattooed, forever on display for the world to see and judge. For people to stare with disgust and pity.

I swallow down my negative thoughts and close my eyes.

No two people are alike.

Everyone has flaws.

I am more than my scars.

I take a deep breath and exhale on three. When I open my eyes, the person I was focused on in the reflection is overpowered by a woman with short curls. Her bright smile welcomes me and her hand beckons me to open the door. I do as I'm asked, sliding right into the building I'd been standing outside of for a good five minutes.

"Melody, right?" The woman wraps her arm around my shoulder and pulls me into the building.

"Yeah, that's me," I tell her even though she's already dragging me inside. "Your flyer never said your name."

She drops her arm from my shoulder as we reach the stairwell. "Celeste Valencia. Everyone calls me Cece. Pronouns are she/her."

We climb the steps until we reach the second floor. Chatter echoes through the stairway from above us. Before I can look up, she pushes the door open and cocks her head for me to follow.

My gaze drifts over the people in the common area sitting with their legs crossed leaning over as they mark up a poster board with big letters. I try to make out the words but a nudge from Cece pulls me away. She drags me through an empty hallway and to the third room on the left.

Taking out her school ID, she swipes it over the card reader and pushes the door open. I walk in as she holds it open and I look around. On the left, there's a raised bed with a desk pushed under it. On the right, it's slightly the same, only the bed is higher up. It's enough for someone to stand or sit comfortably unlike the left side.

Walking over to the bed on the left with mermaid fin patterned sheets, she hops on and crosses her legs. "So you're looking for a roommate?"

"Yeah. I just transferred here."

"A week after the semester started?" Her gaze travels over me and lands right where everyone else's attention always does. She tilts her head, and a smile forms on her lips as she looks back at my face. "Interesting. So you need a room and housing is more than likely not going to accommodate you anywhere."

"I put in for a room, but I didn't get one. They were full and last week, I was sick so I just got to campus today."

Her gaze falls over me once more. She takes her time, assessing my features before it travels downward. Part of me thinks she's going to ask me to spin. Maybe she wants to make sure I fit her standards, whatever they may be. Or she's like my dad and is judging before she gets to know me. Though, I don't really think it's either.

"Do you know what this stands for?" She points to her wall where a five-striped blue, pink, and white flag resides.

A small smile curls on my lips as I nod. "Transgender."

"Cool." She raised an eyebrow at me. "And you wouldn't care about having a transgender woman as a roommate?"

I tilt my head, not entirely sure what that means. I know it's a term but I always forget if it means a man who transitioned into a woman or vice versa. As if she sees my confusion she speaks up. "I was born a male."

Don't trust these gender-changing people. They are what they were born. They'll use it to their advantage.

My dad's words float into my mind and I shake them out faster than they can finish. "As long as you don't care that I like to sleep with just my underwear and shirt we'll be fine."

"Oh, I like you." She chuckles, running her hand along the mermaid scales on her sheets. "Can I ask or?"

She's being polite, making sure I'm comfortable. Not that

she needs to. I prefer being asked. It's a much better feeling than being stared at like a circus freak. "I was born with a missing bone and the scars were attempts to make me normal."

"Normal's overrated."

I smile; if only that were actually true. I'd give anything to just be like everyone else. "If it helps the whole roommate process, I can reach behind and wipe my own ass. I won't need help."

She bursts out in laughter, shaking her head. "I don't think it matters much."

I blink twice, unsure what she means.

Did I do something wrong?

Am I not getting a place to stay?

The negative questions swirl in my head but I stare at her, waiting for an answer anyway.

"To be honest, I'm looking for a roommate for my brother," she shrugs her shoulders, a smile still on her lips, "well, surprising him with one."

"Oh," is all I can say. "Shouldn't he know you're looking for him?"

She shakes her head. "And give him the chance to say no? Absolutely not. He needs a roommate whether he believes it or not."

There's something about the way she says *roommate* that should make me skeptical, but I need a place. Preferably before my dad gets out of his meeting. "Why did you ask about me not caring if you were my roommate?"

"Because I know my brother. If you're not accepting of me, he won't even entertain the idea of you."

That... is a little harsh but I get it. My older brother is the same way.

"Is there any chance I'll be able to move in today?" I ask.

"That depends on how quickly I can convince him." She tips her chin up. "Why?"

"My dad is trying to get me to live at home instead of with strangers," I explain, not wanting to go deeper into that conversation.

"That's fine. I mean, worst case you can sleep here for the night." She gestures to the empty bed on the other side of the room. "So how'd you transfer in the middle of the semester?"

"My dad actually works here." I rub my hand over my arm. "He's the chancellor."

"Oh." I didn't miss the way her eyes widened. "You're Watson's daughter?"

I nod, hoping it isn't too much of a problem. I glance down, shuffling my feet. "Yeah. Is it an issue?"

She chuckles, shaking her head. "For me, not at all."

But that didn't mean it would be for someone else. Stepping further into the room, I trail my fingers along the brown oak desk. A cup of iced tea sits by her open laptop. On the screen is a music app—at least that's what it looks like. I pull out the chair and take a seat, pulling down my sleeves. Not really sure why I had them up in the first place.

My gaze falls back to her as the clicking noise of her typing away on her phone draws my attention. Yet even so, my mind drifts back to the guy on the quad with his bright yellow eyes. They were like an apple pie—no, more like the sun, warm and comforting. There's something familiar about them. Maybe it's because of Sergio, the dangerous yet sexy mafia leader, in the story I'm writing. He has the same color eyes, only they burn with rage... especially when he rescues Aria from her shitty brother who would have let her die to save himself.

"So what are you studying?" Cece's voice draws me from my own head.

"Creative Writing," I tell her as my fingers follow the circular pattern etched into the desk. "You?"

"Psychology," she says.

I glance back at her as she shrugs. Her phone pings and she types back while responding. "My brother's on his way."

Already?

"He should be here in…" she taps her finger on the screen. "About a minute or so. He's pretty good at rushing to my side when I need him."

My palms suddenly begin to sweat and my leg bounces. I shouldn't be nervous; not when Cece is clearly a nice person. Her brother probably is too. But the idea of meeting someone new always has me feeling this anxious.

Two knocks at the door catch our attention after a few seconds of silence.

"Cece, open up," he sounds frantic, out of breath, and more than anything, worried. "It's me."

"He probably thinks I'm in trouble," Cece shrugs with a grin like a person banging on the door is no big deal. She slides off her bed, taking her sweet time.

"Cece?" He calls out again, this time banging his fist.

"Relax," she says, opening the door.

Cassius, the same man from the quad, comes barging in like he owns the place. He looks around until his attention falls on me.

Electricity sparks over my skin as his gaze trails over my body. Heat flushes to my cheeks and my heart does a little skip, but it quickly disappears the moment he glances back at his sister.

His chest falls and his gaze softens. His shoulders slump.

He takes a deep breath and exhales while running a hand through his hair.

"You wanted me to meet your new roommate?" he asks.

Cece shakes her head and places a hand on his shoulder. "Nope. I want you to meet *your* new roommate, Melody."

5

YOUR NEW ROOMMATE

CASSIUS

A simple text has me sprinting all the way to south campus from the opposite direction. I never even replied. There was no reason. My sister needs me, and that's the only thing keeping me from tripping over my own two feet.

I swerve past the students, taking their sweet ass time to get to class. They draw on talking to each other like it's no big deal and I guess for some; it isn't. If I were in their position, I'd be dragging my feet too, but I'm not. This isn't for a class. It's for Cece.

She's usually so sure of herself. For her to change her mind after the person got there means something is wrong.

My legs get there faster than expected, heart pounding with each step. I pull the building door open and hurry up the steps. The moment I get to her floor, I push further until I reach her room.

I'm out of breath, but fuck it.

I don't need air if I end up losing my mind.

My knuckles tap gently against the door.

"Cece, open up," I say, my voice strained and sounding much more desperate than my knock. "It's me."

I move closer, pressing my ear to the door. She's moving around in there. At least I think that's her. Shit. My body shakes, unable to calm the nerves rattling inside. *Fuck, I hope it's her.*

"Cece?" I call out again, pounding my fist this time.

"Relax," she says, opening the door.

I barrel in, ready to deal with whoever is in this room. My gaze surveys the area but stops instantly as it falls onto *her*.

Moonlight.

I stop breathing for a second and look at my sister. Physically, she's fine. No marks, bruises, or any sign of harm. She's even grinning.

My chest falls. I'm ready to sink into a chair and let it swallow me whole. My shoulders slump. I take a deep breath and exhale, running a hand through my hair.

It's hard to keep myself from crashing to the floor. My legs wobble but I ball my hands into fists, trying to ground myself and ease the thumping of my chest.

Cece gave me a fucking panic attack. And for what? "You... wanted me to meet your new roommate?"

Cece shakes her head and places a hand on my shoulder. "Nope. I want you to meet *your* new roommate, Melody."

Melody. Right, my—wait what?

"I thought *you* were the one looking for a roommate."

"No," Cece tilts her head pressing her pointer finger to her cheek. "I never said I was looking for myself."

*This conniving little—*My eyebrows draw together, lips pursed. Cece's trying to look out for me, I get it, but it's hard to simmer my annoyance when she's crossing boundaries. "So you decided to look for me, without even asking me."

"Yup," she pops the 'p' for dramatic effect. "And since Melody just transferred. She's looking for a place to stay."

I click my tongue, eying my sister. "Isn't that what student housing is for?"

"Did you not just hear me? She just transferred. They aren't going to help her."

"They said I have better luck asking around," Melody's voice is soft, reminding me she's in the room with us.

"See! And you have one spare room."

I roll my eyes, crossing my arms. "Yeah, for when you and Declan need a place to crash."

"Where's your heart, Cass?" Cece pouts as she pokes my chest. "A *beautiful* woman is in need and you won't even help her?"

Her true intentions click. Cece doesn't want me to help Melody because she's in need. She wants me to get close to someone. Just like the time she was adamant about the clients I took last month.

It's about time you get a girlfriend.

A scoff leaves my lips and I turn my attention to Melody. Her head is low as her fingers play with one another. "You really have nowhere else to stay? No one you know lives on campus or around here?"

She bites down on her bottom lip, dipping her chin even more.

Fuck.

"No Cass, she doesn't," my sister answers for her. "I'd let her stay here, but I like my privacy."

I let out a deep breath, dropping my arms to my sides. My sister is really lucky I love her and know her all too well. She would never want to leave someone stranded. And although neither would I, the fact that I've been intimate with this particular woman puts a strain on my decision.

I'd like to say fine, knowing that nothing would happen between us. But since her moonlight eyes hypnotize me in a way I can't seem to shake, there's no way I can know for sure it won't happen again. Not to mention the possibility of either of us wanting more when I know damn well I can't give her much. My time, effort, and attention are already preoccupied. I can't make any more room.

Yet, when Melody looks up and her moonlight eyes find mine, there's a silent plea like I'm her only option.

Her only hope.

And I can't ignore the pull tugging at my heartstrings.

I tear my gaze from her and focus on the laptop on top of the desk. "You can move in."

Cece squeals, jumps, and wraps her arms around my neck, pulling me into a hug. My arms wrap instinctively around her.

"She'll be good for you, I can tell," Cece whispers.

There's no guarantee Cece's right. However, she was right about our brother being secretly in love with his best friend, Ophelia. She was right about Ophelia being in love with him back, despite having a boyfriend at the time. And she was definitely right about the fact that I obsessed over finishing a project for a client I barely got to know.

But now said client was here.

Cece pulls away from me, and I look over at Melody.

"I'm hardly ever home, so it'll be like having your own place," I say, hoping it makes her feel a little bit more comfortable than she might be feeling.

A knock at the door keeps her from saying anything. It's our brother, Declan. I know it's him. I can feel his presence near even though he's not inside.

My attention follows Cece as she walks over to the door and opens it.

I stare at a mirror version of myself. Declan grins sporting a pink Redwood University sweater. The black snapback on his head is backward and a basketball rests under his arm.

His gaze drifts to the opposite side of the room and falls onto Melody. Before he can say anything or causally flirt like he usually does, I move towards him. My hand grabs his shoulder and I pull him right out of Cece's room, letting the door close behind us.

"What's up with you?" he asks. It's not like I can lie to him. We have this weird twin bond that no one really believes. When one of us is hurt or feels high levels of emotion, the other can feel it.

I glance over at him. He rubs his chest, eyebrows furrowed. "Cece texted saying you thought he—she was in trouble but I can tell there's something else."

A sigh leaves my lips. "Remember how I told you about that one night?"

He tilts his head and then opens his mouth. "The girl with the short arms and scars you told me about."

I nod.

"Is that her?" His eyebrow raises and I nod once more.

"She doesn't remember me."

His eyes widen, lips forming in the shape of an 'o'.

"Damn… that sucks. Did you even try to ask if she knows who you are?"

"No, I mean I didn't really realize it at first either. But it's her. And I said she could live with me."

Declan glances up at the ceiling like it has all the answers in the damn world. Or maybe he's trying to keep his mouth shut and not say something that he knows will bug me. I never know with him.

"What was it that you called her… Midnight?"

"Moonlight," I mumble.

"Right." He nods, placing his hand on my shoulder. He gives it a little squeeze, but it does nothing to elevate the tension I suddenly notice. "You'll be fine, Cass. You're worrying too much. Think of it as a clean slate. She doesn't know you. You didn't know her to begin with. Now you can do all that lovey-dovey shit you like to do and win her heart."

Yeah. Declan is right—no. No, he's not right because there will be no lovey-dovey shit. I have too much on my plate. Adding dating to the picture will just be a hassle.

I sigh, letting my shoulders drop.

It'll be fine.

Everything will be fine.

He opens the door and I walk back in with him in tow.

"Sorry about that, *Moonlight*." My face drops as he says her nickname. The one I came up with for her. The one I used multiple times the night we spent together.

Her eyes widen with realization, and I can't help but look back at my brother. He's grinning, like the flirt he always acts like.

And it takes so much in me to not punch him right in his stupid face.

6

TOO EARLY TO BE FALLING

MELODY

oonlight.

M The name ripples through my body, shattering every piece right down to my core.

It's him. It's actually him.

Sunlight.

He's real, not a figment of my imagination.

For a long time, I thought he was a dream. A warped memory of the day I visited the school. A daydream my mind conjured after meeting the sweet tattoo artist who had the most inviting smile and gorgeous eyes. The inspiration for Sergio's appearance and kind actions toward Aria in my book.

And here he is, standing by the doorway.

How could I have forgotten his face? Those sunlight eyes must have done more than captivate me. They prevented me from remembering anything else.

"Just one night."

One night that meant more to me than my previous relationships.

I was a fool. An idiot. Why did I kiss him? I shouldn't have done that. I barely knew the guy. He just seemed so nice and I couldn't contain myself. Not when he seemed so genuine. But that didn't excuse the fact that I kissed him without asking—without his approval.

My finger tapped against the glass of water in front of me. I'd been sitting in this bar for hours, not wanting to head back to campus. I was at Redwood to figure out if I wanted to transfer here, not kiss a random stranger. Especially not after I found out my boyfriend placed a bet with his friends about me.

"Didn't think I'd see you here." *I turned at the sound of his voice. Sunlight. A small smile played on his lips, the sight nearly making all of my worries disappear.* "But I'm glad I did."

He did?

"I wanted to apologize for earlier."

I blinked twice, my stomach tying into knots. "Why—what do you have to apologize for? I should be the one saying sorry to you. I shouldn't have kissed you without thinking things through and making sure you wanted to."

He tilted his head, the smile never left his lips even as a small chuckle escaped.

"What?" *I asked.*

He shook his head and crossed his arms over his chest. "I'm just still trying to wrap my head around why a girl like you would kiss a guy like me."

My chest caved in at his words and my gaze drifted to my fingers, nails already digging into my skin. A girl like me?

Different, deformed, ugly.

He didn't mean it like that, right? "What do you mean?"

"I'm just some roughed-up tattoo artist and you're... this," *his velvety voice trailed.*

"Please don't call me porcelain or fragile," *I said.* "It's insulting."

Especially when my parents used it time and time again as a reason for being cautious with me over the years.

A smirk quirked up the corner of his mouth. "I was going to say a goddess with battle scars."

I bit the inside of my cheek, eyebrows furrowing. "Are you making fun of me?"

"No." He moved to the stool beside me and sat down, his body facing mine. His hand dropped to my knee as his fingers sprawled out, sending a wave of heat from under his palm.

I tried not to stare, but I was doing a terrible job at it. The dragon with hollowed eyes inked on his arm down to his hand looked like it was ready to sink its teeth into my skin. I swallowed hard and forced myself to meet those sunlight eyes.

"Not at all, Moonlight." He was so careful with his words.

"You must get girls all the time."

Unlike me who blurted out what came to mind when I was nervous.

"I'm not sure how to take that." He tilted his head, smiling. "Are you calling me a man whore or irresistible?"

I bit down on my bottom lip and shook my head. "Neither."

"Damn." He retracted his hand, letting it fall to his lap.

"What I mean is that you're charming."

"Ah yes." He pursed his lips together, trying to hide back the smile that seemed to be permanently glued to his face. "I mean there's only one woman who planted her lips on me, but I guess I used to get girls back in high school."

"And not now?" I asked, suddenly curious. Sunlight was handsome. His well-defined arms were enough to make me daydream about him lifting me off the ground. The designs on his skin only made him that much more attractive. And then his eyes and smile... that charming and shy, yet sweet smile.

He could have anyone dropping to their knees for him, even after opening his mouth.

"Life gets busy."

"So you don't have sex?" And there went my thoughts, rolling off of my tongue to make me look like a fool.

But he didn't seem to mind. In fact, he leaned closer almost intrigued. "No, Moonlight. I don't. Do you?"

"I mean I have before but not like... nothing casual. When I had a boyfriend we did."

"As in past tense," he murmured.

"I wouldn't have kissed you if I was with someone."

"So, you kiss strangers on a whim."

"No!" I shrieked, and my eyes widened. But there was a playful glint in his eyes that calmed my sudden nerves. "I—I was overcome with an overwhelming sense of emotions."

He laughed, a smile coming to his face and I could have sworn there was a little dimple peeking out from the corner.

"I don't just go around kissing strangers," I told him.

"And I usually don't have to try so hard to erase someone from my brain after one meeting."

Now it was my turn to smile. "But you sit with clients at the bar."

"No. My company is usually only the moonlight."

Silence loomed over us as our gazes were glued to one another. He was something out of a romance novel but if he truly was, right now would be the moment when he leaned in and kissed me. But he didn't.

"You're making me want to kiss you again," I said, my voice soft.

"No one's stopping you." He moved his stool closer. My ankles separated, and my legs parted, letting his knees slide between them as he leaned closer. "But fair warning, if you kiss me again, I might not be able to stop this time."

My stomach flipped at the idea. "Maybe I don't want you to stop."

"That's a very dangerous situation."

"Why?"

"You know why." He took my silence as his sign to continue. "Moonlight, I haven't had sex in a long time. And here you are a beautiful, smart, woman telling me not to stop if we start."

"Is this the part where you tell me we can't and cave into your desires anyway?" I asked. His sunlight eyes revealed every apology, every promise, and every regret he could have possibly had. My hand cupped the side of his face. "Sorry, I've been reading a lot lately."

"Oh yeah? Is that what happens in the books you read?"

I shook my head. "Not always... some just go for it because they know the person. They can read their body language."

He hummed. His gaze swept over me, sending a shiver down my spine. "You mean like how I know that wasn't because you were cold?"

I bit my bottom lip. His attention dipped right down to it. "You're making it so hard for me to say no, moonlight."

"Then say yes."

"If we do this," he sighed, placing his hand on my thighs, "you can't expect anything from me."

"I don't," I reassured him.

"Now I just sound like an asshole." He didn't, at least not to me. I wouldn't ever see him again and I was ok with that. Just this once.

"No relationship. No feelings. We both have our lives," I told him, letting him know I understood. "It's just one night."

"Yeah," he didn't seem too happy about it but he went on anyway, "just one night."

"We don't have to."

He leaned in and brushed his lips to mine. "Just promise me you'll tell me to stop the second you change your mind."

"I won't change my mind."

"Promise me, Moonlight," he whispered against my mouth.

I took in the faint spearmint on his breath and pressed my lips to his. "I promise."

"Then let's get out of here."

Yet, I still forgot him.

"I knew you looked familiar," Cece chimes in breaking Sunlight's hold on me. "You're the tattoo virgin."

Only one person has ever called me that before.

"Have you ever gotten a tattoo before?"

I shook my head, lowering my gaze.

"Oh, well then, I know the perfect guy you should see to help with your virginity."

How could I have not recognized her? Cece looks exactly the same as she did that day. Granted her hair was up but still. I usually pay attention to people. Then again, it was an off day for me.

"I still am," I say.

After that day, I never got my tattoo. The doctors believed it was in my best interest not to. And with my anxiety building more and more, I didn't want to freak out over bleeding too much or getting an infection.

The corner of Sunlight's mouth twitches into a smirk. My cheeks burn because I know he was the only *thing* that marked me that day.

"So, *Moonlight.*" He looks over at Cass like he's waiting for something—anything from his twin, but nothing comes from Cassius.

"Her name is Melody," Cece tells him.

"Melody, eh?" He chuckles, looking back at me. He struts

toward me oozing all the confidence in the world. Had he been this way when we last met? "Declan. It's nice to officially meet you."

I expected his name to be something else. Something much smoother than Declan for sure.

His eyes are golden, much like the sunlight. However, they aren't as bright as I thought they had been. There are flecks of green surrounding the gold tint giving it a darker shade than what I remember.

Declan reaches for my hand with his free one and lifts it. His gaze falls on the scar over my knuckles. His eyebrows draw together for a split second but he quickly recovers and leans down, brushing his soft lips over them.

I spot the dragon tattoo on his hand. However, I thought it was on the other side… Maybe I was wrong? Unless Cassius has the same tattoo as well?

"Why don't you make yourself useful instead of flirting with my new roommate?" The bitter tone catches me off guard, especially since Cass had seemed super sweet earlier when he told me where I could find Campbell Hall.

"Relax, Cass," Declan chuckles. "I'm just welcoming her."

"As *cute* as this is," Cece clasps her hands together, stopping the two from pushing their confrontation any further, "Melody, didn't you say something about moving your stuff in as soon as possible?"

Right, before my father leaves his meeting. I nod in response, unable to find my own words with my hand in Declan's and Cassius' gaze on me.

I should have known I'd see the man I had a one-night stand with at some point. It was during my visit here six months ago we met. But I thought he was older, at least a few years older, and definitely not a student here—nor did I think there'd be two of them.

"Why so soon?" Cass asks. I really don't want to answer that and luckily he shakes his head. "Never mind. It's none of my business. You're welcome to move your stuff in now if you want."

He reaches into his pocket and pulls out a set of keys. Taking one off a keychain loop he walks sideways into the small space beside Declan. My hand moves from Declan's and I grab the key from Cass.

"Won't you need it?" I ask.

He shakes his head, glancing at the watch on his wrist. "The shop was supposed to be open a few minutes ago, so I have to head out but I'll be home tonight. We can talk for a bit then."

Oh. My shoulders drop as a sudden feeling washes over me. Sadness—no disappointment? I'm not sure. But I force a smile on my face.

"Cece and Declan can help you move in," Cass adds.

"And you can come to karaoke," Cece chimes in with excitement. "I can introduce you to everyone."

Everyone? My stomach drops. I'm not good at meeting people—especially not a group of people, which is what Cece makes it out to sound like. There's a sour taste in my mouth as I clutch the key in my hand.

"At most, it'll just be us and Ophelia," Cass mentions as if he's aware of how uncomfortable I feel. "She's practically family."

"She *is* family," Cece corrects him.

I keep my gaze on Cass as his drifts back to mine. His eyes are different from Declan's. True sunlight for sure. But maybe it's the way the sun is seeping through the window and casting its light onto his face. It's almost like his eyes are on fire, ready to burn down everything in their path to see beneath the surface.

He rubs the back of his neck and clears his throat. "I'll see you at the tavern then."

I nod, his words are smooth and dangerous much like his gaze. He turns and I watch him go until he disappears behind the door.

"And here I thought what we had was special, *Moonlight*."

My cheeks burn. He caught me staring at someone else. Not just anyone but his brother. His twin brother. "W-we agreed for it to just be one night."

Declan rubs his finger over his chin. Unlike Cass, his beard has fewer stubbles. "One night? Why the hell would *I* do such a thing like that?"

"Deck," Cece grumbles elbowing him.

I bit my lip, shrugging my shoulders. Honestly, I'm not sure, then again, I'm also not entirely convinced he's Sunlight. Not when they're twins.

"That's stupid," he mutters under his breath. Declan's eyes dart to Cece for a moment before glancing back at me. "So really? Just one night?"

I furrow my eyebrows, watching him for a moment as he waits for my answer. "You tell me, *Sunlight*."

Declan smirks, shaking his head. His gaze drifts around the room like he's trying to figure out how to change the subject. Maybe he knows I'm not entirely falling for his act. "Where's your stuff?"

"At my parent's house," I mumble.

"Which is?" he asks, raising an eyebrow.

"At Watson's lovely home off campus, I'm sure," Cece tells him.

His jaw drops as he blinks twice. "You're Watson's kid... you know your dad *hates* us right?"

Does he? I shake my head slowly.

"Well, no. I'm sorry," he corrects. "That's a lie. He hates Cece and Cass."

"That's because you're his star basketball player," Cece says, sprinkling a little sass into her tone. "But don't even worry about that Melody. You'll be fine."

"Yeah, okay." Declan rolls his eyes. He reaches for my hand and pulls me gently to my feet.

But my knees give out the moment I stand up straight. His arm wraps around my waist. His muscles press into my back, pushing me into him. He smells like a mixture of vanilla and sugar, sweet and comforting. Nothing at all like ink or pizza grease. I glance up at him. His smile is playful, just like the glint in his eyes.

"A little too early to be falling for me, Melody." He lets out a small chuckle as he pulls away.

Believe me, I know.

And yet, I'm afraid I might fall if he is my Sunlight.

7

DREAMS OF A SELFISH BOY

CASSIUS

*"Y*ou're so fucking beautiful, Moonlight," I whispered, my gaze trailing over those curves. My fingers itched to trace and memorize every inch of her bare body. "Lay back."*

She hopped back onto the tattoo bed, her eyes never leaving me. Her chest rose and fell as I inched closer, discarding my shirt. Leaning down, I grabbed her hands and wrapped them around my neck. I wanted her close, as close as we could get. Our foreheads touched. Her lips—a hair from mine.

My mouth brushed over hers. "You remember your promise?"

She nodded, biting down on her lip.

"Anytime you want to stop." I kissed her lips. My hands slid around her waist as I leaned in, pushing her slowly and carefully down onto the tattoo bed. "Tell me and I will."

Her lips pressed back against mine, no longer seeming nervous or shy. No, she seemed to be eager. But I wanted to take my time.

I hovered over her, letting my fingers explore the soft flesh. My grip tightened as she pressed up against me. I needed to keep myself in control before I did something drastic. My selfish desires were getting in the way and I needed to keep in mind this was just a one-night thing.

But at this moment, in our moment, she was mine. And I'd treat her the way I would have treated her if she was my girl.

The way she should always be treated.

A knock at my door grabs my attention. My hand stops moving and I blink twice, staring at a sketch. The details in the eyes and the light shading tell me I had been mindlessly drawing Melody's.

I should have been used to it. I'd been mindlessly sketching details of her from the moment I laid eyes on her. Yet, now that she'll be within reach... I'm not sure I'll be able to keep her only in my dreams.

The door opens and I glance back, catching my brother. He leans against the post, his arms crossed over his chest. His gaze drifts around my tattoo station as if he's never been in here before—as if he doesn't have his own right next door. "I see why you like her."

"I don't like her." I turn away from Declan and close my sketchbook.

"Right," he says, not believing me for one second. And why would he? We're twins. He knows I'm lying. "She was just some one-night stand you hooked up with to wet your dick."

It was definitely much more than that, but what's the point of admitting it when he's more than aware I'd never just *wet my dick.*

"Alright. I like her," I admitted with a sigh. "Melody wasn't just a one-night stand."

"I got that much." He strolls into my station and grabs a pink ink tube off my station. "I just don't understand why the hell you agreed to it."

I shrug my shoulders, running my fingers through my

hair. It seemed easy, at the time, to pass it off as just that. She was a client and according to her paperwork, not from here. However, the moment my lips tasted every single part of her, I was already too deep. Our promise was set in stone. One night. Nothing more.

"If this is about Cara—" I spin my chair to face him, shoot a look, and he stops short, not finishing his sentence.

He knows it is. We both know.

"It's me or this place. It can't be both."

"I can't be forced to choose between this place and someone again, Declan. It'll be this place. You guys. My family. Always."

He shakes his head and grips my shoulder, forcing my gaze back onto him. "The right person isn't going to make you choose. She'll see it's your life. She'll just want to be a part of it and have you be a part of hers."

A smile grows on my lips. The way his eyebrows draw together tells me he can't even believe he said those words. But I understand why he did. "Ophelia has you reading her favorite romance books again?"

"Yeah. She says it's a manual." He rolls his eyes and takes a step back. "So… you're really not going to see where this could lead?"

"We're roommates now," I say. "It'll be better this way. Keep her close, instead of losing her completely."

Declan narrows his eyes. My jaw stiffens, annoyance suddenly flooding through me—his annoyance with me that is. "Who the fuck are you and what did you do with my brother?"

"Funny." I roll my eyes.

"No, seriously because I swear I'm just talking to myself at this point."

I manage to smile, giving him a shrug. "We are twins."

"You're not allowed to be," he waves his arm up and down, "*this.*"

"Sucks to see someone think they shouldn't go after someone they have feeling for, huh?"

"Fuck you." Declan scoffs, lowers his hand, and shakes his head. "But fine. I get it."

I breathe out and stand, placing my sketchbook on the stool. I'm just glad he isn't trying to fight me on this. I know if it were Cece, she'd do exactly that.

"Did she get settled in and everything?" I asked, changing the subject.

He nods, flipping his snapback around. "Yeah. Can you believe she had two entire boxes full of fucking books?"

"Sorry, I've been reading a lot lately."

A chuckle leaves my lips as I remember the apology she once gave me. "Honestly, I wouldn't doubt it."

"She also has a shit ton of notebooks. And when I tried to look in one, she snatched it from my hands like I was going to destroy it." He scoffs, shaking his head. "She's hiding something. Guarantee she's plotting our deaths already."

I laugh. My brother is *almost* as dramatic as Cece but he keeps it under wraps. "Ophelia will probably get to you first."

"She is the death of me with those fucking blue cotton candy eyes." His shoulders slump, but his hand balls into a fist as his gaze focuses on my desk. "I don't know how much longer I can fend those fuckers off her."

"Ophelia can handle her own, Deck," I tell him, but we both know that already. We both *also* know that's not the real reason why he meddles in her dating life. "She doesn't need her best friend to protect her."

"Same goes for me and Cece, yet you still kill yourself to be our support."

It's different. I'm the big brother. Since we were kids, I took care of them. Not mom, not dad… me. When Declan broke his leg, I was the one who sat beside him in the ambulance. When Cece came out, I worked hard to get an apartment because I knew she'd be tossed out.

Mom may have cared for Cece before her transition, but not once did she give Declan an ounce of love or affection. That was Cece, Ophelia, and I. And Ophelia wasn't even related.

"I'm not killing myself to be your support. I'm here so you guys don't have to worry." In fact, I'm finally beginning to adjust my schedule accordingly to accommodate everything in my life.

"Yeah, but *I* remember your dreams, Cass. You wanted to get married, wanted to have your own family. How can you get that if you aren't giving anyone a chance?"

None of that matters to me. Not anymore at least. Those were the dreams of a selfish boy who only thought about himself. No. I'll figure out new dreams once they find theirs.

"Don't worry about me, Deck." I walk over to him and wrap an arm around his shoulder. "I got everything under control."

"I really hope someone catches you off guard and you realize it way too late to back out."

Luckily, that won't happen. The only one who ever did is living right under my roof. And I wouldn't tell him that either. "Help me close up since you've been too busy to pick up a shift."

"No one misses me," he says.

"I miss you."

"You see me every fucking day. We work together at the tavern and here, except for during basketball season." Declan rolls his eyes. "Besides you were the one who pushed me to join."

I did because he loves basketball. Ever since he held one in his hands, playing was all he ever wanted to do. Just like me when it came to drawing. We were good at both, but drawing and tattooing are more my things than they ever were his.

Dragging him out of my station, we walk down the small hall decorated with various photographs of tattoos, drawings, and images we offer. Most are original. Hardly anyone comes in requesting a specific tattoo. Besides, I would rather they choose from what I have than copy someone else's work. Working with a client and bringing something they've always imagined to life is a different kind of feeling. And I love doing it. That's why I hoped Melody would come back... but now she thought Declan was me.

"So, did she ask you about the nickname?"

"No." Declan shakes his head, shrugging my arm off his shoulder. "But she did push back when I asked about the one-night thing so she might already know...Which is good for you. Not everyone catches on to the obvious."

I hum, feeling a slight heaviness in my chest. It's him. He's thinking about Ophelia, and how he believes she doesn't know he's in love with her. I take a deep breath and smile. "At least she's a part of your life."

Loneliness creeps up into my soul and surrounds my heart. My gaze scans the papers scattered over the front desk. It's going to take a while to clean this place up. Declan pats my shoulder and I look up. He smiles at me, pushing me gently.

"Let's get this done so we can find a distraction for our shit mood."

A breathy chuckle falls from my lips. Even though I feel a bit lonely. I know I'm not. My brother knows me better than anyone ever could.

As much of a dick Declan can be, I'm glad to have him.

8

NOT A ROMANCE NOVEL

MELODY

Karaoke night, on a Thursday. I'm not sure that's the best decision for the tavern. Most people I know go to parties on campus to get drunk and flirt with one another. They don't go bar hopping. Most are under the legal age anyway. So to have karaoke on a weekday when most people won't care doesn't make sense to me.

I'm just hoping not many people are here. Crowds are the worst.

Cece walks beside me though, easing a bit of that worry lingering in my thoughts. The strap of her purple backpack slings over her shoulder. Her lips move, but my thoughts overpower her voice for most of the walk. And now that I can see Inked Hearts Tattoos & Piercings, I can't help but want to head there instead.

"You said they're both going to be there?" I ask out of the blue.

"They work at the bar." Cece glances my way, but my gaze is glued to the shop ahead. "You think they're cute, don't you?"

Cute is an understatement. Her brothers are straight out of a fiction novel. The loud and confident flirt—Declan. And Cass, the quiet, possibly brooding, and modest; the complete opposite. And they're not just brothers, but *twins*. That's the kind of stuff I've only read about. Yet, here they are in real life.

How?

Am I in a romance novel and don't even know it? Is this how my characters feel?

No. That's too much to think about. This is real life. Definitely *not* a romance novel.

Girls like me are never the main character or even the love interest. Girls like me would be someone's side character to someone's main—someone like Cece—someone with confidence. I look over, as she glances back at me. Right, I have yet to answer her question.

"A lot of people think they are," she says.

"Just cute?" I ask.

"More along the lines of *I want to sit on your brother's face* and *he can force me to my knees any day*." She shrugs. "Take your pick."

"Yes," I find myself blurting out.

That's not even a choice, Mel.

"Disgusting." Cece laughs, shaking her head. "So anyway, all those notebooks. What were they for?"

A grin tugs at my lips. "The small ones are journals. The one with a sunset cover is poems. The bigger ones are ideas and stories. Most are unfinished though. And about half of them are just too pretty to write in."

My dad sees it as a waste of a notebook, but they're cute and I'd rather use them for something important. I just haven't figured out what.

"Oh? What kind of stories do you write? Or, or... better

yet, what are you working on?" She raises an eyebrow at me like it's some sort of interrogation.

It's not.

"Well…" I trail off needing a moment to think. "Right now I'm writing a mafia story. It's about Aria who ends up getting taken as collateral because her brother has been trying to kill this guy named Sergio. He ends up going to kill her brother but she steps in front of him before Sergio can and Sergio takes her because he thinks her brother is a piece of shit who would just let his sister die, which spoilers he was going to."

Cece's laughter cuts me off. "Breathe, Melody." I do as she says and she laughs again. "Now continue."

"Where was I?" I look around searching for the place I left off in my head. "So yeah, Sergio takes Aria and she ends up as his *prisoner* but not really. He's done this before and got hurt so he tries to keep her at arm's length and yeah."

"And how far into the story are you?"

"Um, I just got to the part where he takes her because I had to figure out his backstory and the previous person he did this with broke his heart because she loved someone else. She's going to make an appearance too."

Music suddenly catches my attention and it's only now that I realize we are right outside of the tavern. Redwood Tavern to be exact. At least that's what the name etched into the glass says.

"You should publish it one day. Sounds interesting. I'd read it," she says, opening the door.

A warm, giddy feeling bubbles inside me. At least I'll have one reader. One friend. No one else really knows I write. My family does, but they've never read my work and my dad thinks I should follow in his footsteps. Become a teacher and work my way up.

But that's not me.

Following behind Cece, I take in the blue and yellow lights illuminating the place. There are hardly any people. Two people stand behind the bar and one person sits on a stool, brushing their hair off their shoulders.

I can't tell the twins apart—who are behind the bar. One of the boys, who I assume is Cassius, because he seems more responsible, is replacing the empty alcohol bottles on the shelf.

The other leans forward, his arms crossed as his elbows press against the counter. He's smiling at the woman in front of him.

The one who I think is Cassius notices us. He smiles and waves in our direction. Cece takes my hand, pulling me along with her.

I slide onto the barstool as the one I believe is Cassius moves in front of me. The soft gaze in his eyes lets me know I'm right. He is Cassius.

"Promise it's not always this dead." He glances over my head but continues, "We just opened up an hour ago."

A smile breaks out on my face. "It's fine. I prefer it this way to be honest."

He nods, looking back down at me. "Hope you don't mind Cece ditching you."

Huh?

I look around and sure enough, Cece's no longer next to me. I didn't even notice her hand slip from mine. Turning around, I spot her by the stage, setting up. Right, she said she's the DJ.

"That's ok, I can just stay here with you." I spin back. Cass is staring at me with a curious gaze. Heat flushes into my cheeks and I'm suddenly unsure of myself. "If that's ok."

"You can do whatever you want," his voice is smooth and sweet like honey. His eyes stay on mine, almost like there's a hidden meaning behind them.

"Planning on singing?" The sound of his voice fills my ears but his lips don't move. It's a little deeper and more playful. Declan no doubt. I shift my gaze to him. He stands beside Cass in a white t-shirt instead of black like his brother. "I assume you can sing. Your name is Melody, after all."

Is this a test?

Someone slides onto the stool beside me. My shoulders tense aware there are way more people around me than I'd like. One or two people I can handle. Three or more, I start to shrink back into my little bubble.

"I bet she can sing better than you, *Avey*, that's for sure."

"Fuck you, alright, Ophie." Declan smirks, flipping the person beside me off. "I can sing."

"Yeah, okay," she says as I look over. She rolls her eyes, keeping her attention on him.

"Ophelia and Deck always argue," Cece's voice suddenly whispers against my ear, making me jump. When did she come back? "It's like their foreplay."

Oh. Were they…

"They aren't together," Cass says as if the question was written over my face. I focus on him, letting Declan and their friend fall into the background. "Everyone thinks they are."

"They might as well be." Cece scoffs, placing her hand on my shoulder. "You should sing though. Cass is up first tonight."

"Really?" he asks.

"Yup. Deck went first last week and I did the week before."

Cass mutters something under his breath and gives me a small smile. "I'll try not to make your ears bleed."

Something tells me he couldn't even if he tried.

Cece's hand falls from my shoulder and I turn, continuing to ignore the two beside me still bickering back and forth. Cece finds her way to the booth, making an announcement for the four people in the tavern. But the two beside me cheer anyway, and I find myself joining in.

"Now give it up for your bartender and my single older brother, Cassius!"

He walks over, dragging his feet as he takes his time. His hands are deep in his pockets. My gaze never leaves him as he hops onto the stage and makes his way over to Cece. He says something to her before he moves to the microphone stand. His fingers wrap around the mic. He closes his eyes and takes a deep breath. Shai, If I Ever Fall In Love seeps through the speakers along with Cass's voice.

He starts with the spoken words, captivating me with every syllable but what really has a hold on me is his singing voice. He's stroking each note like he's done this his entire life. And maybe he has.

I can't help but watch him get so into it. His eyes closed, one hand on the mic, the other on his stomach. My throat is suddenly dry, but my body relaxes. He's good. Really good. Talented for sure. My body sways to the sound of the music blending with his voice. I think this might be my new favorite song, his version.

He even manipulates the high 'friend' note to work with his vocals.

Sergio should totally sing to Aria.

I don't take my eyes off of him for a second, not even when his eyes open and meet mine. But he quickly clears his throat and looks away as he steps back from the mic.

A smile forms on my lips and I clap for him, just like the two beside me.

Ophelia leans over. The smell of cotton candy suddenly surrounds me. "I see you've fallen for his voice."

I bite my lip, shaking my head. "No, I'm just surprised."

"They're good. All three of them. We used to have this cover band back in middle school called Ophie and the Dicks."

Laughter bursts from my lips. "Was it because they were dicks?"

Ophelia moves back, giving me space to finally take her in. Her blond wavy hair drapes over her shoulders. Blue eyes glisten with a hint of yellow from the lights.

"I mean, they were but no. It was because, at the time, I was the only vagina. They all had dicks." She shrugs with a smile. "Cece's always been my girl though."

"And Declan?"

Ophelia looks behind the bar and my gaze follows, landing on Declan who is dipping cotton candy into a martini glass.

"He's my best friend," her gaze drifts back to me, "always will be."

There's a hint of sadness in her tone, one I understand wholeheartedly. And suddenly my stomach stirs with guilt to know her secret without her even mentioning it.

"You drink?" Declan asks as he slides Ophelia the martini glass.

"Not really, no," I say.

"Want one of those then?" he asks, pointing to the drink now in Ophelia's hand. "It's a mocktail. Ophie doesn't drink much either."

"You look like a lavender lemonade kind of girl," Cass's smooth voice rings. I look over at him, just as he lifts the part of the bar table and walks under. He lets it drop from his hand

and moves inches behind Declan. He tilts his head. His gaze burns my skin as it flickers over me. "Maybe a strawberry cucumber mojito."

That did sound pretty good.

"Cass can read people," Ophelia vouches. "He's the one who came up with my cotton candy mocktail."

I wonder if he'll let me read him one day.

Shaking the thought from my head, I smile. "Alright. Surprise me then."

9

COMPETE WITH YOURSELF

CASSIUS

Melody might have drank two strawberry cucumbers, but she downed three lavender lemonades like they were nothing. And to be fair, it *was* just juice. No alcohol at all. Not like the glass of bourbon, I let sit behind the bar for too long.

"Declan told me she's the girl," Ophelia says as she presses her chest up against the counter. My gaze stays glued to her face, the smile on her lips growing wider. Sometimes I wonder if she does it on purpose like she thinks I'll sneak peeks like Declan does.

But I don't because, unlike him, I see her as a friend. More like a sister than anything. "I figured he would. He tells you everything."

"He also told me about the one-night stand. Does Cece know or just us?"

To be honest, at this point, I am not even sure. For all I know, everyone in our circle has heard about it. Maverick, our cousin, has for sure. He and Declan were the first I told.

Kind of hard not to when I work with and see them every day. And now her, thanks to Declan, but I have yet to tell Cece about sleeping with anyone unless Declan mentioned it after I left.

"I don't think it matters. Cece's still trying to push me into a relationship."

"I heard. Roommates." Ophelia chuckles. She lifts her glass and takes a long sip of her drink. "But that doesn't mean you can't have another night… or more."

"It means I definitely can't. For one, she's my new roommate. Two, I don't have time for any of that."

"You can make time." Ophelia smirks, wiggling her eyebrows at me as she places her drink down. I roll my eyes and grab the empty glass. I lift it to my nose. Alcohol.

"Declan needs to stop caving in or you'll love the floor again."

"It was just *one* drink," she pouts, clearly not wanting to talk about the time she wanted to stay on my bathroom floor by the toilet and sleep. "Besides, I'm staying with Deck."

Until he pisses her off, no doubt.

"Where is he anyway?" I ask.

She turns her head and I pull away before her hair can smack me in the face. "Setting your girl up on stage."

"Melody isn't my—"

Chills run through my body at the sudden voice coming from the speaker. My gaze lifts to the stage where Melody stands behind the microphone stand. Her mouth moves to the lyrics of Alessia Cara's "Here."

She's feeling the music with her eyes closed. I almost believe every word she's saying even though they aren't hers. My head bobs to the beat of the song. It's one of my favorites if I'm being honest. And she's managing to hit every note flawlessly.

Melody doesn't let the words slip when she needs to take a breath. She follows through like she's done this plenty of times before. She seems confident up on that stage. The lights don't seem to blind her as she stares out toward the crowd, ignoring the words on the screen. She knows the song, and she's owning it.

Maybe I should add a music note to the pages flying off of the typewriter.

The song she sings makes it seem like she doesn't want to be here, but it's clear as day, she belongs on the stage.

If I could keep Melody up there, I would. She doesn't bow her head or bite her lip like she's hiding from the world the way she did the day I first met her.

A lot can change in six months.

And the idea of getting to know this Melody sparks something in my chest. Developing something more with her…. Where I can see all phases of her and she can meet every part of me—even the person who wouldn't have let her go that night.

But… only when things in my life slow down, of course. Or maybe she'll understand? No. I shake the thoughts from my head.

This isn't a time to be romantic.

It never is.

Melody's song fades out and I clap for her, watching as she smiles. Brushing a strand of hair behind her ear, she ducks her head and reverts to her less confident self.

"That's my roommate!" I call out, cheering and clapping even louder.

She lifts her head, looking in my direction. Her smile

grows. Pride swells inside knowing I brought *that* to her face. She walks toward the bar but gets stopped. Once, twice—multiple times by our usuals. Congratulating her, no doubt, as they should. Melody was magical up there.

I want to hop over the bar and wrap my arms around her.

But I barely know her.

Yet, that doesn't stop my brother from doing so. He takes it a step further, lifting her off her feet and spinning her in a circle. Melody's shoulders bounce and although I can't hear it, I know she's laughing.

"Something tells me you want to make her yours, even if you can't admit it," Ophelia's voice slaps me from the scene. My gaze falls from them and down to my hand clutching the empty glass.

"How about I get to know her first before I confirm or deny that?" I hand her back the empty glass and she takes it without question.

"Just don't wait too long." Ophelia winks. She turns from me, sliding off the stool. "You wouldn't want to compete with yourself."

You mean the man Melody possibly thinks my brother is.

My shoulders slump as her words and my own cast a shadow of doubt over my head. Declan's gaze is on me, but I don't bother to acknowledge him. Instead, I walk over to the customers at the other end of the bar.

I just want this night to be over. So I can get home and shut myself out from the rest of the world.

"I didn't know T-Rexes still existed." Laughter comes from one of the men, stealing my attention. "Can she even scratch her head or wipe her own ass?"

Anger bubbles through me. I slap my hand against the

counter, grabbing his attention. My gaze narrows as I look him up and down.

"Leave," I grit through my teeth. My body shakes as I try to keep myself calm on the outside.

"What?" he asks like he hadn't just heard me.

"I said leave." My fingers grip his collar, pulling him up to his feet and close to my face. "Get the fuck out. Now."

His nails claw at my hand. "What the fuck is your problem?"

"We don't tolerate ableist bullshit." I shove him.

"It was a fucking joke. Relax." He stumbles back with a smirk, dusting himself off. "Didn't mean to offend you or your retarded friend."

10

JUST A JOKE

MELODY

A sudden outburst catches my attention. Declan's hand slides into mine. He pulls me with him through the thick crowd circling the end of the bar. The smell of liquor lingers in the air and broken glass shatters in the distance. My skin crawls, heart racing. I don't want to go anywhere near the commotion, but I have no choice. We're already pushing through. Declan's grip loosens as we get closer to the middle. My hand slips from his and I wrap my arms around myself. He reaches for someone, pulling whoever it is off of the other on the ground.

"I said get the fuck out. You're not welcome here. Ever."

My eyes find Cassius. He doesn't try to push Declan away or go around to get to the other guy. He huffs, shoving Declan's hands off, and turns, pushing his way through the crowd.

My chest tightens, fingers twitching with need. I want to follow him but my feet are rooted to the ground. I don't know him like that. For all I know, Cassius needs time alone.

"Alright, show's over!" Declan calls out. "Pack it up and go home."

Declan sighs, looking over at the man on the floor. His hand is on his nose, and crimson trickles from between his fingers.

"Now, what exactly did *you* do to piss Cass off?" Declan grips the man by his collar and pulls him up to his feet.

"Nothing."

"Was it about my sister?" he asks, keeping his hand wrapped around the man's collar. "The girl behind the DJ booth?"

"No," the man spits in disgust. His eyes widen realizing he made a mistake. "The short-arm girl."

I flinch at his words as Declan turns his gaze to me. The man's attention follows.

"You mean her?"

Of course, he means me.

The man nods. "It was just a joke."

"What was the joke?" Declan asks, tilting his head. "I want to know. Jokes are funny right?"

The man looks at me, then back at Declan like he's afraid he's about to get hit for the second time… or however many times Cass might have punched him.

"Declan," I say, lowering my gaze from either of them. "Just leave it be."

"No. Go on," Declan's practically growling. Neither of these men know me and yet Cass was quick to come to my defense, as is Declan. "Tell me, what was the fucking joke."

"Deck," I hear Ophelia call to him. "She said to leave it alone. Just toss him out so we can clean this place up and go home."

Declan grunts. "Fuck, fine."

It's only then that I look up and watch as Declan shoves the man past us and toward the exit.

I cross my arms, rubbing my hands over them. My eyes close as my throat tightens. I take a deep breath, trying to keep the tears away.

It was just a joke.

Words that once hurt me try to make their way to the surface, but I shut them down before they can emerge fully. They usually don't bother me. At least, that's what I say to myself. I think I've just grown numb to them throughout the years. And the truth is, their words can't hurt me more than I've already hurt myself.

Once upon a time, I actually believed them.

But it still hurts, especially when it draws a crowd.

"You okay?" Ophelia asks. I open my eyes and nod as she smiles at me, placing a hand on my shoulder. "I can handle Declan. It's hard to cool his hot head down. Would you mind checking on Cass? He went through the back."

She points in the direction of the door directly in front of us. I nod again and make my way. I push the door open, spotting him instantly.

Cassius is pacing back and forth, mumbling under his breath. His fists pound against one another. He doesn't even know I'm here. The door behind me slams shut and it's only then that he looks up at me.

"Declan threw him out for you," I say.

His gaze softens. He doesn't say anything, he doesn't need to.

We stand there in silence. I'm not sure exactly what to say other than, "Why'd you do it?"

Cassius furrows his eyebrows. "What do you mean?"

"Why did you get into a fight with him? We just met. I'm

not anyone important." I sigh, glancing down at my feet. "I'd ask if you were just doing it to get in my pants but—"

"Nobody deserves to be treated or spoken about badly for just being."

He feels bad for you.

The sudden thought swirls in my stomach.

"I hit him for being a jackass and talking shit. No one should ever talk about you the way he did." He huffs, running his fingers through his hair. "I would have done the same if he said anything about my sister."

"But she's your sister. I'm nothing."

"Is that really what you think about yourself, Melody?" He asks, taking a step in my direction.

I swallow the bitter feeling coursing through me, unable to form any words. He draws closer, erasing the space between us along with the air in my lungs.

"You think that you're nothing?"

I lift my gaze. Tears blur his vision, but I can still tell he's tall by maybe a foot. I'm not sure, it doesn't really matter to me right now. Not when his sunlight eyes are focused on mine.

"I know I am." I'm not even sure my words came out but when he shakes his head I know it did.

"No one ever told you otherwise?"

My back presses to the door. The cool metal calms me, helping the tears simmer down. "Just.. my family and my friend."

His arm rests above my head as he leans. "No boyfriends?"

I don't think my ex even knew I thought that way. He showed me affection, but that was only when he wanted me around. When he wanted attention. And that only confirmed those thoughts. I shake my head in response.

"Look, I get it. We just met." His warm hand cups my chin, lifting my face closer to his. "But I already know you're wrong."

"I'm not," I whisper, trying to keep the tears from resurfacing.

"You are." His gaze scans my face and drops down to my lips. A soft smile forms on his face before he looks back into my eyes. "You're not *nothing*, and I'll prove it to you."

I want to believe him.

But everyone has their reasons… and part of me wonders if this is a cruel joke like they'll humiliate me in public to have a laugh. Or maybe a bet of some sort. Which brother can get the disabled girl to fall for him first?

I've read so many different versions of *this* kind of story and I don't want to be a character in it.

Not again.

"I told you it'd be fucking easy," I heard Jay chuckle. I was ready to climb out from under the bed and surprise him with the cake I made, but a feminine giggle stopped me from doing just that. Bare feet drew closer. The bed dipped as she sat on it. Luckily the frame kept it from trapping me—even though I was trapped. "So... you're not dating her?"

He scoffed, moving between her legs. My chest tightened. What was he doing in here with her? "Nah. It's just a bet I made with the guys."

A... A bet?

"As if anyone would date someone like her."

"And she fell for it?"

"Yeah. She thinks we're a real couple—in love." He laughed, chipping pieces of my heart. I swallowed down the pain. "Even met her parents."

A moan comes from her mouth. "Sounds pretty serious."

"I promise it's not." The sound of sloppy kisses against skin made my stomach swirl. I covered my mouth with my hand. "Maybe I could get you into her daddy's graduate program at Redwood."

"Wait, her father works there?"

He hummed. "He's the chancellor. And if you're good I'll make sure to tell him all about you."

She giggled again and I tuned out the rest, covering my ears while I waited for them to be done and leave.

I close my eyes and take a deep breath. "Please let me go."

To my surprise, Cassius drops his hand. His foot crunches on a piece of glass as he steps back and his scent flies away with the wind.

When I open my eyes back up, Cass is standing a foot away. His hands are in his pockets. "I'm sorry. I shouldn't have invaded your space."

"It's okay," I say, straightening my back. We're off to a terrible start and it's been a long day for both of us. "Can we start over in the morning? Get to know each other then?"

Cass nods. "Yeah. It's been a crazy day. You must be tired after moving in and everything."

I nod, fiddling with my fingers.

"You don't have to be nervous or anything, Melody. I don't want you to feel uncomfortable around me. Especially since we're going to be roommates. We can start over and take things slow."

A smile creeps up on my lips. Maybe it's the way he can calm my nerves or the way he speaks with such a soothing voice, but it makes me feel better.

Like all of my worries and fears are valid.

And that, in itself, is something more than anyone else has ever given me.

11

TELL HER THE TRUTH

CASSIUS

Melody and I haven't talked.

We've yet to cross paths in about a week. I've been busy, dealing with the tattoo shop and my slip-up at the Tavern. Luckily, the manager wasn't too hard on me.

Green eyes stared at me from across the bar. I was sure he'd be angry, but instead, he looked at me with sympathy. Mr. Monroe leaned against the shelves, hands gripping the wood for support. He sighed, shaking his head. "You're lucky he didn't go to the police. He still can you know, and it'd get this place shut down."

I sighed, resting my elbows on the bar. Guilt nips unbearably at my skin "I wasn't thinking."

"You should be though. As an employee, you should know better than to start fights. And as someone who officially owns a shop, you need to keep that in mind."

"So, I'm not fired? I thought you'd be mad."

"Anyone else would." He shifted the weight on his feet and crossed his arms. "But I've known you since you were a kid, Cass.

You wouldn't just start a fight without a valid reason. So what happened?"

"The asshole said ableist shit about someone I know." I leaned forward, tapping my fingers together. Just thinking about it made my blood boil. "Called her the R-word."

"Alright." He pushed off of the shelf and sighed. "Next time just kick him out. No fighting."

I perked up. "So I get to keep my job?"

"Yeah, in exchange for extra work hours. But if this shit happens again, you're gone."

That was fine. It wasn't like the Tavern was my only source of income. Mr. Monroe made sure of that when he handed me the tattoo shop. Still, those extra hours were helping out with my expenses.

He sighed, resting his hand on my shoulder. "Let's talk about those extra hours and how to make them work with your schedule."

Working more at Redwood Tavern wasn't much of a hassle. It just left me with less time to rest. Less time to sleep. Less time to focus on my classes. No time to talk to my new roommate and come clean.

Still, I drag myself into the tattoo shop, ready to get to work. The bell above the door rings and a head pops out of one of the rooms.

It's Maverick—Our cousin.

He's sitting on his stool, rolling it out into the small hall. He tilts his head, combing back his hair with his fingers.

"I was wondering when you were gonna show up," he mentions, not that he needs to.

I know I'm late for my shift.

"Had to talk with one of my instructors about an assignment I failed to turn in on time."

The line across his forehead creases, eyebrows drawing together. "Thought you were good about finishing them."

"I am." Mostly. It's not like I meant to turn it in late. Last night, I had stayed at the tavern past midnight, cleaning up, and forgot it was supposed to be turned in before then. "This week's just been hectic."

"Cece mentioned something about a fight at the Tavern." Maverick rolls the sleeves of his sweater down, covering his tattoos. "And a new roommate."

I hum, partially glad I don't have to explain much since Cece did it all for me. "Yeah, Mr. Monroe has me working extra this week because of it."

"He pretty much lets you guys run the place when you're working. You guys might as well own it yourself or ask him to make you co-owner."

No way. I'm already struggling as it is to pay for my tuition, the mortgage on this building, and all the extra utilities for my place and here. Being a co-owner or anything above the title of a bartender is just too much on my plate. "I don't think I can take on more responsibilities."

"Have you given any thought about my offer?" He raises an eyebrow at me.

"I've considered it." I shrug, moving over to the front desk and shifting through random papers. Truth is, I haven't thought much about splitting the business in half since he brought it up. We are the only two who really work our asses off at Inked Hearts. Cece, Declan, and even Mave's sister Astraea help too, but Maverick has been my partner since Mr. Monroe passed the shop down to me and let me make it into my own.

"And?"

I can't give Maverick an answer. I'd rather not burden him

with the shop financially. Yes, it'd make my life ten times easier with less coming out of my pocket, but Maverick is family. Even if he's asking to help, I would rather him not deal with the same headache.

Before I can answer, I sense Declan. The bell behind me rings as the door swings open.

"The crew's all here," Declan wraps an arm around my shoulder. From the corner of my eye, I see him grinning. "What are we chatting about?"

"Business deals." Maverick huffs out before his hard gaze falls back on me. "So?"

"Still thinking about it," I say.

"He's not going to do it," Declan chimes in. "You know Cass almost as much as I do."

Maverick shakes his head and sighs. "Don't be an idiot. Let me help run the shop. I already invest and handle shit when you aren't around."

"Barely."

"Because you never take a day to just fucking chill." Maverick stands from his stool and kicks it back into his tattoo station. "You're working too hard, Cass."

"I'm fine."

"Mave is right, you need to chill. And get laid." Declan shakes my shoulder. "Maybe your new roommate can help out with that."

"Not gonna happen," I tell him as Maverick mutters something under his breath and rolls his eyes. "What? Don't tell me you think I should too?"

Maverick tilts his head, looking between Declan and me. "Doesn't matter what I think. I know it'll happen."

"I'm not having sex with Melody again," I grumble.

"Wait, she's the same girl?" Maverick questions.

Shit, I hadn't meant to say it *that* loud. "Yeah."

"But she might think I'm the one she slept with because unlike him," Declan adds, "I made her remember."

Maverick scrunches his face in disgust. "I don't want to know."

"We didn't share the same pussy, if that's what you think. I mean we did come out of the same one but no. Cass and I never had sex with the same girl. That title only applies to you."

A groan comes from Maverick. I don't blame him for not wanting to fall back into *that* conversation. Maverick didn't know Ophelia and Declan had sex in high school before she transferred schools. He also didn't know, at the time they dated, that she was the girl Declan always raved about during the holidays. Ophelia joining us for Thanksgiving our senior year as Mave's girlfriend was the icing on an already rough year for my brother.

"So why would she think it's you?" Maverick asks.

"I called her moonlight," Declan shrugs, "Guess it triggered her memory or something."

"And neither of you cleared it up for her?"

Declan looks over at me. A silent question brewing in his eyes. "I haven't. Cass lives with her. Figured he told her already."

"I haven't had the chance to even see her, let alone clear it up."

"That's still fucked up."

"She'll figure it out. We might look alike, but we aren't the same." Declan adds.

"You know, I expect this from you, but Cass, really?" His gaze catches mine. Green eyes stare at me full of disappointment. "She deserves to know the truth, it's her right. What if someone did the same shit to Cece, my sister, or hell even Ophelia? Would you think it was right?"

No. When he puts it like that… no. It isn't the right thing to do at all. Even if she didn't really think it was Declan, telling her the truth would clear up any confusion.

"So that's your advice," Declan mocks, "tell her?"

"Take it or leave it." Maverick rolls his eyes. "Think about my offer. I get it. You think it's selfish to put that kind of pressure on me, but I want this. The job, the responsibility. Yeah, I'm planning on being a teacher, but tattooing is what I want, and I can become an instructor. We can even bring on apprentices, so they know the ins and outs before starting."

He's really thought about this… I nod, shoving my need for full control aside. "We can talk about it more another time."

My words put a small smirk on his face before he turns from us and heads back to his station.

"You gonna tell her then?" Declan asks, turning his attention to me.

I bump my shoulder into his. "Whenever I get the chance. I don't have a choice, do I?"

"Nah. When Maverick puts it in our face like that… kinda makes me feel like shit." He reaches and rubs the back of his neck. "Especially since the way she looked at me before."

I nod, letting my bag drop from my shoulder. I grab the strap with my hand and place it down on the front desk. "Yeah. It's best if we come clean."

It is the right thing to do, after all.

12

SOMEONE LIKE ME

MELODY

A ria tried to inch away from him, though... that was impossible with his body pressed to hers. His hand was on the wall and the other was holding his drink. *"Neither of us can have an opinion on one another if we don't know each other... and you could have killed me. Another easily would have." She tried to step to the side instead.*

"Cute." He placed his other hand against the wall, drink still in hand as he disabled her from moving away. His gaze met hers, dark with the intent of scaring her. "I am dangerous, but that doesn't mean I'm a monster."

"Even Lucifer was an Angel."

His mouth curled into a smirk as he leaned in, eyes fluttering shut as he inched closer to her lips.

"Get out," he whispered as he moved away from her and finished his drink.

"I'm sorry," Aria squealed and scurried from his office.

Inspiration has been leaking through my fingertips the entire morning. Sergio might not be happy with me since he's still stuck with Aria two months later in the book, but I already have my idea for the next chapter.

I crack my neck, moving it from left to right, and sit up straight to relieve the ache of slouching. Sure, it might be comfortable, but it's terrible for my back. My fingers fall back onto the keyboard. However, before I can even type, the laptop is slowly closing. I glance up, seeing one of the twins. Declan, I think. He's leaning over the table. One finger pressing the back of my laptop with his gaze on me, a playful glint in his eyes.

"You hungry?" he asks, lifting the screen back in place. "Or are you busy?"

I peek at the clock on my computer. It's already noon? I didn't realize how long I'd been in the library for. My stomach suddenly growls like it's angry that I hadn't noticed it was past my usual lunchtime. "I can eat."

"Good. We can hit up the dining hall."

"Right…" I feel bad asking, but if I don't, I'll never know. "Which one are you again?"

A chuckle leaves his lips. "I forget people don't always catch on quickly."

"Well, I haven't seen either of you since I moved in. So, it's kind of hard."

"Declan," he tells me. "My dragon tattoo is on the right and Cass's is on the left. Our eyes are different too."

He points it out like it's the easiest way to tell them apart and I guess, if you look close enough it can be. But at first glance or a quick look, it'd be tough to tell them apart.

"Cass also never wears a snapback." He points to his head. "And I usually have a basketball in my hand."

He shrugs his shoulders and my gaze drifts down to his

arm. Sure enough, he has an orange basketball tucked right under.

Something in his eyes tells me he's not just saying this so I know. He's trying to make a point. For what though?

Still, I pull my laptop closer and make sure my document is saved before I close it. "You said dining hall, right?"

"Yeah. We can head downstairs, or we can take a trip to Hillside."

"Isn't that all the way on north campus?" I ask.

"Yeah, but it has the best food if you ask me."

That might be true, not that I'd know. I have yet to step foot on north campus. All of my classes, much like the next one in a little over half an hour, are all on central campus. "I don't think I'd have enough time if we do that."

"What's your next class?"

"Shakespeare," I say, grabbing my laptop and placing it inside my book bag.

"You won't be missing out."

My attention snaps right back to him. As if I'd skip a class just to go eat with someone. *Sunlight* or not, I can't skip any class. Not all of my credits from my old university transferred. Meaning, I might have to take winter classes over the break just to make sure I can graduate on time next year.

As if he can read the look in my gaze, he holds his hands up in defense. The ball is still securely held by his side and elbow. "Alright, fine. Downstairs it is."

I zip up my book bag and grab the strap, but a small tug on the other keeps it rooted. Looking to see where the other strap may be trapped, I catch his fingers curled around it.

"I can take it for you."

Shaking my head, I tug at the strap. "No thanks. I can carry it on my own."

Declan tilts his head. A smirk curls on his lips. "Ok, but the offer stands if you change your mind."

Maybe it's his attitude or the fact that I know he might not be the man I once slept with, but the fluttery feeling in my stomach hasn't returned.

Or maybe it's the fact that he wants to help when I'm not asking for it.

Most would see it as a kind gesture. I just see it as him trying to help the disabled girl who doesn't need it. My mind rounds back to the idea of bets. A sour taste spreads in my mouth. I don't like it. "Why are you here?"

"It's a library," he says, finally letting go of the strap. "Didn't know I wasn't allowed to be in one."

I shake my head and sling the book bag over my shoulder. "That's not what I mean."

"Why don't you explain it to me then." He raises an eyebrow, keeping his gaze on me.

A student passes by us, crinkling paper in their hand. It sounds louder in the silence of the library. "You came up to me."

"Yeah," he says like it's no big deal, "because I know you."

"You don't though."

Declan sighs. "Not yet. I mean, you're my brother's roommate and if Cece has it her way, you'll probably be her friend in no time if you aren't already."

According to Cece's texts, we are. We've talked non-stop since our first meeting. We're even graduating together next year. Cece and I are definitely shaping up to be friends.

"You're not answering my question. Why are you here, talking to me, asking me to go eat with you?"

"Because I want to. Is that so hard to believe, that someone actually wants to get to know you and be friends?"

"Yes." I look him dead in the eye. He furrows his eyebrows as if he's shocked by my sudden cold demeanor. "No hot guy who should be in a romance movie would ever want to be friends with someone like me or would have even had sex with me for that matter."

"To be clear, that wasn't me."

My mind goes blank. My body doesn't move. Air is trapped in my lungs, and I might be exaggerating, but I think my heart literally stops.

It's like he's ripped off a wax strip, leaving me to process the facts.

He isn't Sunlight, which I kind of already figured. But, he waited to clear up the mistake.

At least he was telling you now.

After the fact.

He could have twisted the truth out like toothpaste at the end of the tube, but clearly, that isn't his style.

"We," I draw out the word, "didn't have sex?"

Declan shakes his head. "No. I only called you Moonlight because I was hoping it'd push Cass to say something. Didn't think you'd really question which one of us actually slept with you."

"*Cassius*... as in my new roommate," I try to process. I'd agreed to room with the same man I had sex with and neither thought to tell me sooner?

"Why wouldn't I think it's you? You're twins."

Logically, one would think they are the same person. So yeah. I'm not stupid. It's just a complicated situation. They look alike. So, of course, I'm going to believe him when he calls me *Moonlight*.

"Because," he starts, letting out a sigh. "Outside of hookup culture, when you're intimate with someone that shit stays with you. You have this connection."

I draw in a breath and purse my lips together. My grip tightens around the strap of my book bag. I want to smack him so bad.

It's not even funny.

Instead of smacking him, I exhale.

"Be mad at me," Declan catches my attention. His gaze is hard, unmoving. "Never talk to me again if that's how you feel. But don't blame Cass or take it out on him."

"Why not?" I ask. The truth of the matter is, he could have told me too, yet he chose not to. He *should* have told me. We live together!

"He's beating himself up already. Work, school, everything. And I think he really likes you… But I know my brother. He's going to think he's not worth your time or that he doesn't have what it takes to juggle everything plus a relationship."

"Shouldn't he be saying all of this himself?" I ask. Or better yet, shouldn't I be the one to decide if he's worth my time?

Declan let out something between a scoff and chuckle. "Doesn't mean he will. I know him like I know my left nut."

The more he talks, the more I wonder why I didn't realize it before. My *Sunlight* was kinder with his words and took time to answer. Declan doesn't do that. He says stuff like this instead.

"Are you just saying this so I date your brother?"

"No, that's Cece's job. She's the matchmaker." He laughs. "That's why you're his roommate."

Really?

He won't even entertain the idea of you.

Of course. I should have noticed that, especially how she's

always asking if I've gotten to talk to Cass and the way she slips him into every conversation.

"So, what do you expect me to do?" I ask, shifting from one foot to the other.

"I don't expect anything." He shrugs. "I want you to be easy on him. That doesn't mean you *have* to be."

And yet, I feel as though that's the case.

"You shouldn't have kept the truth from me."

"I know, I'm sorry. Probably not as sorry as Cass, because he's been hard on himself lately, but I am sorry." Declan holds his hand out to me. The table stands in between us, still keeping us at arm's length. "Start over?"

I sigh, not bothering to reach out for his hand. He's too far for me to grab it. "Fine. But you're going to have to come around for an actual handshake."

He glances down at my arms as if he almost forgot and nods. "What about a hug?"

"Maybe when we're friends," I say as he rounds the table. He holds his hand out again and I give it a small shake.

"We will be. Trust me on that."

13

LEFT TO BE IN THE MIDDLE

CASSIUS

I drag my feet toward home, backpack swung over my shoulder. If I time it correctly and knock out the moment I hit the mattress, I'll have about two hours of sleep before having to head out. My sights land on a gray duplex. Both sides mirror each other in every way, except for the doors. The Black one on the right and the white one to the left, my place.

My neighbor, Mrs. Maria Monroe, stands in front of a sign on her lawn. She tilts her head. Her silvery locks are tied up in a bun. I smile, coming up beside her, making sure my footsteps are loud enough for her to hear.

"Good afternoon, Mrs. Maria," I greet her in the only way she'll let me. The only time my siblings and I ever tried to call her Mrs. Monroe, she threatened to throw a chancla at us. And as Hispanics, we know never to mess around; especially with a chancla involved.

My gaze assesses the sign she's looking at.

For Sale.

"You're moving?" I ask.

"What did you think?" Her thick Puerto Rican accent slides through her broken English. She places her hands on her hips. "All of these college students. Quiero nada de eso." *I want none of that.*

If I was her age, I wouldn't want to deal with any of it either. "But you were okay with me moving in."

"Sí, porque tienes un gran corazón. You have respect." *Yes, because you have a big heart.* She looks over at me. The wrinkles on her face shift as she smiles. Then she sighs, shaking her head. "Estos niños no lo tienen." *These kids don't have it.*

Sadly, she's right.

No one knows what respect is anymore. They want it but don't know how to get it. Some think they're entitled to it but can't give others the same regard. "Have people already made you an offer?"

"Claro que si. Con el dinero de sus padres." *Of course, with their parents' money.* "If someone takes this house, I want them to take care of it, como mi esposo y yo hicimos todos estos años." *like my husband and I have all these years.*

I get it.

Mr. Monroe worked hard to build this property. Originally, the side I live on was meant for their daughter, but she didn't want it. And since Mr. Monroe has known me since I was a kid, working at his tattoo shop under the table, mostly cleaning up.

"¿Conoces alguien que necesite un apartamento?" *Do you know anyone who needs an apartment?*

Not entirely. Maverick has a condo apartment with his best friend, Nikolaus, and Cece's best friend, Xylina. Declan and Cece are pretty much situated in their dorms. The same goes with Ophelia and my cousin Astraea. And then there is Melody…

"I can ask around."

"Bueno, that's good. ¿Y tú cómo estás?" *And how are you?*

I shrug my shoulders. "I'm fine. Can't complain. Busy as always."

"¿Y la muchacha que yo visto?" *And the girl I saw?*

"She's my new roommate," I tell her, "Cece thinks I'm lonely."

"Your sister is always up to something." Mrs. Maria chuckles. "Well, I'll leave you. If you find someone, me avisas." *Tell me.*

Wrapping an arm around her shoulder, I give her a small side hug. "I will."

She moves, letting my arm drop, and heads inside. I head over to my door and do the same.

I'm greeted with the colorful lyrics of W.A.P., the sweet scent of baked goods, and the sight of my roommate holding a spatula to her lips as she sings and drops down, shaking her ass.

I cross one arm over and rest my elbow on it for support as I bite down on my knuckles, trying to keep my laughter at bay.

Her tight leggings don't hide the curve of her hips or that peach round ass I once had the privilege to grip. The sweater, however, conceals the way her back curves slightly, which gives her ass more than enough attention.

She's cute and comfortable.

I like this side of her.

"Wow," I say, dropping my arms to my sides. Melody snaps up, straightening her back. She turns slowly, her eyes slightly wide with a hint of horror. "I can't believe my roommate thinks I'm a whore."

"How-how long were you standing there?"

"Just for the final drop," I shrug, unable to drop the smile from my lips as I fix the strap on my shoulder. "Don't mind me, though. I'll leave you to your performance."

I walk past the kitchen where she stands by the stove and head off to my room, dragging my feet.

"Wait," Melody calls as the music coming from the kitchen speakers stops. "I made some cupcakes; do you want some?"

I turn to her, knowing I should say no—especially with the way I'm struggling to keep myself up. "Not right now. Maybe later though."

"Oh," she lowers her head, fidgeting with her fingers. "Okay."

Does she have to look so disappointed?

I don't like the way the corner of her lip curves downward or how her gaze shifts to her feet. It's just for a bit anyway. "You know what, I changed my mind."

Sleep can wait.

Dropping my bag in front of my room, I walk over to her. "We still haven't been able to have our talk."

Melody is quiet. She doesn't move an inch. I'm not sure what's going on with her, but part of me is itching to make it better whether or not it's my fault.

"If you still want to get to know each other," I add.

Her head tilts up—moonlight eyes shimmering, yet there's this cloud of emotions obscuring the light of her soul.

"Is everything okay?" I ask as worry bubbles up my stomach.

She nods her head and turns from me. I don't ask her again. I want to, but I'll wait until she's ready.

"Will you tell me everything?" she questions, making her way back into the kitchen.

I follow her. My gaze trails down brown waves, and right down to her—I snap my attention right back to her head. "Anything you want to know, I'll tell you."

She hums, grabbing a tray of cupcakes from the counter. I get a whiff of chocolate and my mouth waters. I'm ready to sink my teeth into one of her delicious treats.

But I can't, not yet.

Melody walks over to the couch and takes a seat. She places the tray down on the coffee table, grabbing one of the cupcakes. I sit down beside her, turning to face her.

She does the same but crosses her legs and leans back on the armrest so she's facing me.

"You and your siblings are close?" she asks, but it's more of a statement than anything. Although she's spent only one night with us, I'm sure she's got the sense that we are.

Still, I answer, because I told her I'd tell her anything she wants to know. "Yeah. We are. For a long time, it was us against the rest."

"What about your parents? Cece said she's not in contact with either of them."

I hum. She's digging for the hard questions already. Or at least, it'd be hard if it were one of my siblings. Guess that's the burden of being the oldest; having to tell our childhood over and over again. "My dad left when we were young and my mom wasn't the best."

Melody nods, encouraging me to continue. "She wasn't too fond of my brother. Said he looked too much like our dad."

"But you're twins."

Yeah, I didn't get it either until one night when I heard her complaining on the phone. "He has my dad's eyes and facial expressions... the way he acts... it all reminded her of him. She also wasn't approving of Cece when she came out."

"My dad doesn't like my brother either," Melody mentions.

"You have a brother?"

"Half," she clarifies, but it doesn't matter. A sibling is a sibling, half, adopted, or whatever, they were family. Her fingers pick at the corner of her cupcake. "My dad loved his mom, but she broke his heart and my mom picked up the pieces."

"So he doesn't like your brother because of his mom?"

"It's... a mutual thing," she says, a little uncertain. "My dad doesn't like him because he sides with his mom and he doesn't like my dad because..." She picks more at the corner of her cupcake and then shakes her head. "They have different views on things."

"And you're left to be in the middle." My gaze drops to my hands. "I get it. Been there. I was mom's favorite, so I only got to see all sides of her."

A cloud hangs over us, silence stretches across the couch, and for a moment, I feel myself caving.

"Cupcakes help," Melody says, pulling for my attention.

My gaze drifts to her. Her eyes are full of worry like she hates where this is leading. And to be honest, I do too. She holds out her cupcake to me, as far out as she can, and lifts it.

She's cute.

I can't help the smile that forms on my face. I lean in and take a bite, keeping my eyes on her. Closing my eyes, I take in the sweetness exploding on my tastebuds. *Damn. Either she's just that good and talented, or I got it bad.*

Swallowing the last bit down, I open my eyes and look at her. She's staring at me, biting down on her bottom lip.

"What?" I ask, sitting up straight. My gaze darts between

her eyes. I want to know what lies behind them, what's going on in her head. "Do I have some frosting on my face?"

She giggles like a schoolgirl and nods, pointing to the corner of my lip. I reach up and swipe my thumb across, cleaning it.

"Want to taste it?" I ask, knowing she hasn't taken a bite of her cupcake just yet.

Melody blinks twice. A blush creeps up those pretty cheeks of hers. "I lost my virginity at a tattoo shop."

I choke on my saliva, coughing for relief. "Wait what?"

"I'm sorry! I didn't mean to make you choke again."

Again?

Wait... "What do you mean again?"

"Declan saw me in the common area earlier." She doesn't need to explain anything else. I know exactly where this is headed.

I shouldn't be surprised. Declan isn't the type who would purposely lead someone on. He's careful. Flirts but makes sure they know it's all talk and nothing more will come of it. I'm just shocked that he went out of his way so soon to come clean before I could.

"I should have told you the moment he called you Moonlight."

"Why didn't you?" she asks. There's a hint of sadness and maybe a bit of attitude. I don't blame her. There's no excuse I can give her.

She has every right to be disappointed.

I should have been forward about it.

Sure, she seemed to be in awe of Declan when he came in and part of me didn't want to break that sweet look on her face. But I gritted my teeth through the entire exchange, hoping maybe she'd see through it.

But how could she when she didn't even know us?

Still doesn't.

"In your head, what was your reasoning?" she adds.

A sigh leaves my lips. Honestly, I have no idea where to begin, so I try my best. "We agreed to one night and if you thought it was Declan, maybe he'd be able to give you everything you could want…everything you deserve."

"But you don't know me, Cassius." Her words are firm, just as her gaze on me is.

"You're right. I don't. And I'm sorry. I really am. I should have corrected Declan the minute he made you think that. It was shitty of me to do. I just… I know I can't give you whatever it is you want."

The silence between us grows, but our eyes are locked onto one another. It's almost like she's trying to find some truth to them.

"All I want right now is to be on good terms with my roommate. It's a little weird to not see you even in passing."

"To be honest, it's been an off week for me." I rub my palms over the fabric of my pants. "Usually, I'd be around after eight. Except Thursday through Saturday."

And thank fuck for that, because this week isn't even over and it sucks ass.

"Just don't get used to the baking. Today's been a good day for me, so it's my treat to myself." She looks over at the cupcakes. "I shouldn't offer you one, but maybe Declan's right about starting over."

I lean back, smiling at her. "What happened today?"

"I pushed through and finished writing three chapters."

She's a writer.

That explains all the notebooks Declan complained about.

Though, now I have no doubts that he's probably right: she's plotting our deaths.

"Three chapters? I can't even write three pages for my English class."

"It's different." She shakes her head. "It's like… drawing for class and drawing for fun."

Now *that*, I understand. When my art teacher used to have us create something, it'd take me hours just to finish one piece. But when I did it for myself, for fun, I sped right through it like it was nothing.

"I guess that makes sense. So you like to write, about what?"

She shrugs her shoulders. Her attention drifts down to her cupcake like she's shy. "Just stuff. Mostly fiction. Love stories."

"Tell me about them."

"You…really want to hear about them?" Melody glances up like I've just told a kid I'd buy them a whole candy store. It fills my heart with a bit of sorrow knowing that someone might have not cared to hear anything she had to say. Every time she talks, every time her pretty mouth opens, she has every single ounce of my attention. I *want* to know what she has to say, what she thinks—even if it doesn't make sense to me.

"I wouldn't be asking if I didn't."

Melody bites down on her bottom lip, suppressing her smile. It takes every ounce of me not to reach over and pull her lip from her teeth. She doesn't need to hide.

Not with me.

"Go on, Moonlight, I'm all ears."

14

IT BROUGHT ME HERE

MELODY

Cassius takes slow and steady breaths. His chest rises and falls as his head rests on the couch. He didn't seem to mind me talking his head off. In fact, he paid attention and even apologized when his eyes drooped. But exhaustion caught up with him, forcing him to cave in.

We didn't get to talk much about him keeping the truth from me or how he punched someone at the bar, but we made progress. And that's something.

Maybe next time we could dive into those conversations.

For now, I'm too fixated on the way he looks. He seems peaceful like the couch is a pile of warm, snuggly cotton. I shift, trying to make myself comfortable. The couch isn't unbearable, but it sinks a little too much for my liking.

My head rests against the cushion, but my hand moves on its own, reaching for him. I want to touch him, trace the lines of his tattoos like I did before, and wrap myself in his warmth. But I can't.

I wonder if Aria has this problem.

When Serglo awakes, yeah. I can see her having this problem. However, Aria would definitely have already touched him if he was sleeping.

So why can't I with Cassius?

Because you're not her.

I lean over, letting my finger brush along the tattoo on his hand. He doesn't move or wake, so I continue my quest. Following the scales of the dragon, I move closer and continue to trace around the charcoal clouds. Or maybe it's just a shadow? The tail disappears under the sleeve of his shirt.

How far up does it go?

I lose my balance and my body tips over. His arm wraps around my waist, keeping me from tumbling off the couch.

"You should be careful," he mumbles in a low, sleepy tone. I turn my head to look at him. We're much closer than I thought. If I dropped my forehead, it'd come into contact with his lips. His eyes are still closed, but he opens his mouth again. "I can feel you staring."

"Have you been awake this whole time?" I ask, keeping my voice down.

"If you're asking if I felt you touching me, I did."

"Oh."

The hand that I'd been tracing my fingers on grips mine gently. He places it on his chest. His heart beats against it, tapping my palm. "Go ahead and explore, Moonlight, I'm all yours."

His words reach my core and I want to take him up on his offer. I want to survey every inch of his body. Last time, I only got a glance. My hands barely got to find every inked design on him. I was way too preoccupied with his touch on every inch of me. And now he's here. I can do that.

But I won't.

Aria would.

Aria would take the chance to press her lips to his.

But, I'm not her.

She's fiction.

I'm real.

Backing away, I retract my hand from his. "No, it's okay. You should probably go to bed though."

"I don't think I'll be able to sleep without your soothing voice."

A smile grows over my lips. *He's such a smooth talker.*

"I'll record it for you, you can play it on repeat."

Cassius hums. "Appreciated."

Neither of us move. He seems content with the idea of sleeping in a sitting position on the couch instead of lying down. But I highly doubt he'll wake up feeling rested. I get off the couch first, grab the empty cupcake tray we gobbled up and head for the kitchen.

"Hey, Moonlight?"

"Yeah?"

"You didn't really lose your virginity to me, did you?"

I let out a small chuckle. "No, Cassius. I, unfortunately, gave that away years ago."

"Why unfortunate?" he asks.

"Let's just say he wasn't worth it, and I was better off waiting."

"I'm sorry, Moonlight."

I smile at the nickname he gave me. I'm sure he thought the same thing when I gave him his. We hadn't exchanged names, but his eyes lit something inside me of that day.

"Don't worry about it. Honestly, I'm glad it happened."

I wasn't happy about the situation. The way my ex and I got together was messy. But what relationship isn't? In their own way, relationships are messy and chaotic, but in some cases, relationships are a beautiful mess, like an abstract painting. No one truly understands it but the people involved.

But that wasn't what I had with my ex, and it took me forever to realize it.

"Why's that?" he asks.

There were a lot of reasons why I was glad it happened.

I opened myself up. Let myself be present in love—blinded, but present. He brought out the worst in me and with the worst I realized: what I wanted, what I didn't, how I should feel, and what I deserved. My ex took, and I gave. He barely tugged, and I lost the war, but I gained something I needed more than love.

The confidence to not care what others think or say about me. People will stare regardless so why should I let fear hold me back?

Sure, it's a fickle feeling and I find myself down every now and then, but I don't purposely hide my arms like I used to.

And looking back, my relationship took me on a journey. It pushed me to do something I never would have had the courage to do before.

"It brought me here."

"To me?"

I chuckle. "Yeah, I guess."

"Doesn't sound too convincing. You're hurting my feelings, Moonlight."

I place the tray down on the counter. My phone buzzes in my pocket and I take it out, placing it down. I glance at my phone and sigh, eying the messages on the screen.

Speak of the devil and he'll blow up your phone.

JAY

you seriously left school?

I thought you were joking

Babe?

Come on Melody text me back

I fucked up.

I'm sorry.

I miss you.

If my ex, Jay, was really sorry, he wouldn't have gone along with the bet his teammates made. He would have told them to fuck off, or at least let them know he changed his mind.

But no, he went along with the bet until I found out. If I knew he wasn't just trying to get in with my dad and Redwood University, I'd consider it. But I knew better. I flip my phone over, ignoring him.

Cass's presence moves behind me, hands on either side of mine. He lowers his chin to my shoulder. His breath tickles my ear. My body shivers and I close my eyes, enjoying the sudden closeness of his mouth. "Whatever the reason is, I'm glad it brought you here too."

Cassius reaches over and I swear he's about to spin me around, but instead, he grabs the empty tray.

"I'll take care of it," he says, pulling away.

My hand rests on my chest, trying to ease the beating of my heart. This man... It's like he's trying to kill me.

Though I guess it's fair since I choked him... twice. Unintentionally.

"Okay," I manage to stumble the word out. My gaze finds

him over by the sink. "Can I ask you a few things before we go to bed?"

He glances over, places the empty tray into the sink, and turns on the faucet. "Sure, what do you want to know?"

"The situation at the bar..."

"I thought I explained the bar situation the night of."

"But what happened after with your boss... with the customer?"

A heavy sigh comes from his lips as he rolls one sleeve over his elbow and then the other. "The customer isn't allowed back in the bar and I had to do extra hours at work."

"Oh," I say softly, my gaze dropping to my feet. "I thought you were just trying to avoid me."

"Why would I do that?"

"So you could keep up with your lie," my voice drops lower than it'd been before. My heart shrinks. I shouldn't have said it, but his steps move in my direction and his feet are suddenly an inch from mine.

"Melody... that's not..."

I glance up, waiting for him to continue—needing him to finish his sentence.

Cass runs his hand through his hair and places his hand against my shoulder. It's warm, comforting, and almost like he's trying to get my full attention. Not that he needs to. He already has it. "What I did is inexcusable. But it has nothing to do with you and everything to do with me."

"I-I don't understand."

"I-" he begins, taking a deep breath, "I've been hurt in the past."

"We've all been hurt before, Cassius. It's not an excuse to lie." My voice breaks. Tears fill my eyes, blurring my view of him. "To make me think your brother is the person I slept with. It's not fair to make me believe something that isn't true."

I wipe the tears threatening to fall down my face. Being upset or even angry won't do us any good. "I don't want to go through that again."

My gaze meets his. Worry fills those sunlight eyes. They're not shining as bright as they should. They're dull, almost… almost like he's breaking. He takes my hand, pulling me into his embrace. A mixture of vanilla and cedar wood surrounds me with comfort.

"I'm sorry, Melody. I mean it. For lying, making you believe something that isn't true. I'll make it up to you. I swear."

His hand runs along my hair, soothing the parts of me that are angry. His words are sincere, his actions seem it too.

But so did Jay.

I push the negative thoughts from my head. Comparison never got anyone anywhere. Cassius isn't Jay.

Taking a step back, I force a smile onto my face. "I'm going to go to my room."

A disappointed glint flashes across his eyes, but he nods anyway. Silence eats away at the moment between us. I shift on my feet. I should go, but I hate the way he seems so down. Moving toward him, I place my hand on his shoulder and rise on my toes. My lips brush gently over his cheek for a second before I step back again. "Goodnight Cass."

He blinks twice, a smile curving on his lips. "Goodnight, Moonlight."

He brings his attention back to the sink. I turn and head to my room, giving him one final look before I enter.

Cassius is deadly.

I thought I could fall for Declan after one interaction. But living with Cassius and being around him every single day…

I am definitely going to drop.

And if I am lucky, I won't smash into pieces.

15

IT'S NOT A DATE

CASSIUS

Melody hasn't come out of her room for the entire week. At least, not when I'm around. I'm not sure why and it's been making my skin crawl. I haven't done anything, at least I don't think I have. We had talked about the issue of me lying. Was that not enough?

CECE

Just knock on her door.

Easier said than done. Then again, if my sister was here, she'd barge right in with no problem. I take a deep breath. Work is in less than an hour, but I want to make sure Melody and I are on good terms before I head out.

Before the negative thoughts eat me alive.

"Melody?" I call out.

Nothing.

Pressing my ear to the door, I can faintly hear clicking like a keyboard or something.

"Sergio!"

Who the fuck is Sergio?

I shouldn't be listening in. Whether she brought someone into the house or not is her business. But I don't hear any footsteps. Just her squealing a bittersweet sound if there is someone else pulling those sounds from her lips.

Her squeals stop for a moment, but her voice doesn't. "Oh. oh. No."

Melody giggles, and there are more clicking sounds. I'm not sure what exactly I'm listening to, but it sounds like she might be alone.

"Oh my god."

Her words bring me back to that night; her naked and spread out on my tattoo bed with her lips parting as she withers under me.

Fuck.

Blood rushes south and I reach down, pressing on my dick, hoping it'll ease the sudden ache. I shouldn't be listening in on my roommate. I *should* be heading to work because she's busy. Yet, I can't seem to move and my dick twitches, urging me to stay.

I try to ease the ache a little more.

Hot chocolate, autumn leaves, centipedes.

Those do the trick. A bit at least. I glance down, making sure it's not as bad or noticeable. *I should just leave her be.*

My knuckles don't get the memo, though, and tap on her door.

A chair in the room scratches the wooden floors and her footsteps grow louder.

"Hey, Melody?" I call out, hoping she can hear me.

"Yeah?" The door opens.

Melody peeks out. Her moonlight eyes gaze up at me. A pair of black oval glasses sits on the bridge of her nose. Her

Redwood University hoodie covers her up like a blanket midway past her thighs. The rest of her legs are bare, aside from those cozy snowflake-patterned knee-high socks.

My heart hammers in my chest, air gone with just the sight of her.

Fuck. Me.

I definitely should have left her alone.

"Is everything ok?" she asks as my gaze drifts back up her body.

"Yeah. I think." I rub the back of my neck, trying to keep my eyes from falling from her face again. "Are we good?"

"What do you mean?"

"Well, I haven't seen you all week. You're always locked up in your room."

"You're never home when I come out for food or go to class." A smile curls on her lips. She's too cute for her own good. "I've been writing."

"Oh yeah, that's right. Aria's story. How's that going?"

"Sergio just got shot."

My mouth parts slightly. *Right, her character's name is Sergio.* She nods, not giving me time to respond. "Aria was trying to grab a book and shook the bookcase, which dropped a shotgun that was hanging from the wall. It fired when it hit the ground, shot through the wall, and grazed his stomach."

My face scrunches. I can't even imagine how much that must have hurt. "Sounds painful."

"He's used to it." She shrugs and I can't help but smile.

She talks as if her characters are real people and I guess they are in a way, to her. Much like my drawings are alive to me... just in a different way.

"Do you want to go out with me tomorrow?" The words leave my mouth before I have time to really digest them. "To like the store or something, I mean. Since you just moved in. Figured maybe you need some things to get settled and feel a bit more like home."

Smooth Cass, real smooth.

"We could go now," she shrugs, glancing back into her room, "if you want. Aria and Sergio can wait."

I shake my head. There's no way I'd drag her away from what she loves doing. Besides, if we leave now, it'd be a quick trip, and I want more time than that with Melody. "It's fine, I know how important they are to you, and I work soon."

"Do you ever take a break?"

Laughter erupts from my chest. The question always comes up and no matter who it is, I answer the same way. "No. I like to keep myself busy."

"So Cece says," she mumbles under her breath, but I catch her words anyway. "I can keep you busy."

That she could.

I ignore the thought my dick conjures up, and tilt my head, watching as her eyes slowly widen in realization. Red creeps up her face. Her pouty lips spread open and I think this might be one of my favorite expressions from her.

"Relax, Moonlight," I say, unable to hide my smile. "I know what you mean."

"What if we go tomorrow then? We make it a day thing."

If we did, it wouldn't necessarily be a day thing. The shop opened up early today and ran until night. Plus, the tavern closed even later. I usually tried to sleep as much as I could since we opened up late on Sundays.

But her round eyes plea behind those sexy as fuck black-rimmed glasses. It doesn't help that her hair is tied up in a ponytail. My dick needs to stop thinking for me because all I want to do is stay home from work, wrap my fingers into her hair, and nibble on that one spot at the base of her neck that makes her whimper.

"Sure." I clear my throat, shifting to keep the bulge in my pants from being seen. "Anything you want."

"What time will you be back tonight?" she asks.

"What time do you want me back?" I counter.

"I'll cook dinner late and we can eat together if you're back before eleven."

A home-cooked meal, made by Melody, just for me... how can she expect me to say no to that?

"Sounds like a plan," I say.

"You can text me if you can't make it."

I could... *if I had her number.* We've been roommates for weeks and I still don't have her number.

I reach into my pocket, pull out my phone, and hand it to her. "Gonna need it before I can do that."

Melody smiles and takes my phone. She holds it close to her as she types. She bites down on her bottom lip, suppressing a laugh, and hands the phone back to me.

I glance down, seeing the messaging app open.

MOONLIGHT

We can both shine bright, like the sun and the moon.

Looking up from my phone, I catch her glancing at hers. "Don't be surprised if I text you when things slow down at the shop."

"I look forward to it." Melody smiles but refuses to meet my gaze. She turns and heads back into her room, closing the door behind her.

There's still time before I have to leave but I head out

anyway. If I plan on making it back for dinner, I have to make sure certain things are in place.

"CASS HAS A DATE TONIGHT!" Cece squeals from outside my tattoo station. It's all she can talk about and at this point, I'm just tired of correcting her.

It's not a date.

Dinner with my roommate is just that. There's no dating or romance involved. It's two people who live in the same place, eating together.

"I don't believe it," Maverick chuckles. I'm not sure, but I assume his door is open. It usually is when he doesn't have a customer.

"I believe it," his sister, Astraea responds. Normally, Rae is too busy with her photography to work with us at Inked Hearts. But every once in a while, she'll stop by, even if it's just to listen in on Cece's gossip. "Cece is never wrong."

"Wait, is that why he wants me to cover for him at the Tavern?" Maverick asks.

A chair rolls across the marble floor and halts by my door. I don't draw my attention from the stack of business cards on my desk. No need to when I know it's him.

"You seriously have a date tonight?"

"It's not a date," I say, not hinting at any sort of emotions— at least, I hope. "Melody asked what time I'd be back. She's making dinner and wanted to eat together."

He scoffs. "That's how it all starts. Expect your favorite food."

"She doesn't know it."

"Neither did Xy, but a *loudmouth,*" he makes sure to yell the last bit out, "decided to tell her the first night she moved in."

Maverick is right. Cece more than likely already told Melody what I like to eat. Well, at least things with her are different than whatever was happening with him and his best friend's girl.

"How are things going with *that* situation?"

"Nothing. She's living at my place. After a long debate with her and Niko, I got her to agree to take my room while I crash on the couch."

An argument sounded like a better term. Niko and Maverick might have been best friends, but ever since Xyli moved in with them, things have been rocky.

I don't know all the details, just the second-hand knowledge from my sister. Xylina, Cece's best friend, wanted to take the next step in her relationship and move in with Nikolaus, her boyfriend. She's nice and all, but I know more than anyone why Maverick tries to keep her at arm's length.

"You're going to torture yourself," I tell him. "They're exes. Aren't you afraid they'll get back together?"

"Not really."

I glance over the moment he shrugs. Everything about Maverick says he isn't worried one bit. And that's a surprise… unless something is going on. But knowing Maverick, he won't say a thing and I don't press him on it.

"Anyway, I'm just warning you in case it happens," he says, "I know you. You fall quickly and hard. You might already have feelings for her after that night."

"I don't." I'm not sure who I'm trying to fool more: him or myself. Ever since our night together, I busied myself with finishing not just one, but several tattoo pieces for her. Then when I woke up to her touching me last week, all I wanted was her hands on me. She's bleeding her way into my skin and I can't seem to stop myself from letting it happen.

"Right," he says, clearly not believing me. "I just want you to watch out. You don't need another Cara."

Ah yes. *Her.* The only woman I ever let into my heart and she ripped it open from the inside, letting the pieces fly and blood drip all over the place.

"Melody isn't like her."

"Cece seems to think the same. All I'm saying is you don't know Melody well yet. None of us do. There's a chance you can still get hurt."

Somehow, I highly doubt Melody could ever be *that* cruel. Still, I nod.

"I know. I'll be careful."

My phone vibrates and I glance over, catching the screen light up with a message.

MOONLIGHT

My parents want to take me out for dinner.
I'm sorry. We still have tomorrow.

My lips press into a thin line—stomach clenching. I shift the business cards and ink bottles around on my desk, busing myself. "Well, it doesn't matter anymore. She canceled."

"Take the night off anyway." Maverick sighs sensing my disappointment. "Sounds like you could use it."

Maybe… now I just had to find something else to fill my time with.

16

A RESCUE CREW

MELODY

assius has yet to text me back.

It's been an hour since I messaged him about the last-minute change. It isn't like I meant to cancel on him. I had no choice. Not with my parents being adamant about going out to dinner with them.

I still don't understand why.

"How's school been, sweetie?" my mother asks. She presses her elbows to the table, fingers intertwined as her chin rests on top. She's in her usual midnight blue dress and heels. Black pearls hang from her neck and matching earrings dangle on a gold chain. My mother usually doesn't do dinner at a restaurant unless it's important, especially not after work.

"Good, considering it's still the first month." I lower my gaze to the half-eaten plate of pasta.

Maybe Cass wouldn't mind leftovers...

Does he even like pasta?

"That's good. And your roommate, is she nice?"

"My roommate is usually busy working," I say, not

mentioning that my roommate is a guy. My mother wouldn't care, but my father—if he finds out—will freak out.

"Hopefully we'll meet her one day," my father says, keeping his attention on the plate in front of him. "Maybe you can invite her for Thanksgiving break."

"Maybe, but they probably have plans with their family."

"Oh sweetheart," my father chimes in again, "that reminds me, we ran into Jay the other day."

"Oh." I glance away, avoiding eye contact with either of them. Jay is not someone I want to talk about, especially with my parents. They adored him far too much, I don't have the heart to tell them what he did and that we aren't together anymore.

"He said he had trouble getting in contact with you, so I invited him for dinner."

"Here?" I nearly shriek.

"Yes, it's not a problem, right?" my father pretends to ask when the truth is he doesn't care. "I figured you missed him anyway."

Not like you do.

I miss my imaginary friends as a child more than I miss Jay. But I won't tell them that. Jay is like the son they never had—that my mother doesn't have.

Shrugging my shoulders, I glance over at my phone. Still no word from Cassius. Does it really get that busy?

Would he have canceled on me if I hadn't?

My phone vibrates on the table. The screen lights up and I take a deep breath. My stomach flutters, but it quickly dies down the moment I see Cece's name instead.

CECE

How's your dinner date with your parents, or
did you lie?

My eyebrows draw together. Is that what they thought? The idea doesn't settle well in my stomach. I pick up my phone, typing back:

My parents wouldn't take 'I have plans' for an answer.

And apparently, they invited my ex.

Their only assumption was that I was going to be stuck on my computer, wasting time. They didn't understand. And I guess that's my fault, in a way, for not showing them just how much I love to write.

CECE

Need rescuing?

I hold back a chuckle. Hopefully, it won't come to that. Maybe Jay won't even show, but with my luck, there's a slight chance he will.

Not sure yet, but I'll keep that in mind.

"Melody, why don't you put your phone away," my father suggests from across the table. "You seem distracted."

Nodding, I do as he asks and slide my phone off the table and onto my lap.

My parents both move their attention behind me. A soft smile comes to my mother's lips. My father pushes his chair back and stands.

A familiar cold touch lands on my shoulder. My muscles tense and my jaw tightens.

"It's good to see you again, Mr. Watson." He doesn't move from beside my chair. Instead, he leans over, shaking my father's hand. "Thank you for inviting me."

"You know you're always welcome," my mother smiles at him.

Jay takes a seat beside me and finally lowers his hand from my shoulder. I refuse to look in his direction, even as his gaze drifts over me.

"I tried contacting you," he says. There's an edge in his tone, but he layers concern on top of it. "To make sure you were okay and settled in."

My hand clutches my phone. I can't believe he's here and that my parents invited him to join us. My leg shakes under the table. He shouldn't be here, but he is.

For what?

To butter up my father so he can get into graduate school at Redwood. Who knows? Not me, that's for sure.

"I'm fine. Settled in and everything," I manage to grit out.

His arm comes around my chair and it's only then that I look in his direction.

Jay's dirty blond shaggy hair falls over his forehead as he turns to me. His blue eyes are like the ocean, deep and mysterious at first glance. But he's more like a polluted lake; shallow and full of trash.

"That's good," he pulls me into his space.

I press my hands to his chest, keeping us at a distance. It's not much, but it's enough to catch his attention. He looks down and furrows his eyebrows.

"Is everything okay?" my father asks from across the table.

Anger rises in me. Heat rushes through my veins. He could

have asked before inviting my ex. I stand, nearly knocking my chair over. "I have to use the restroom."

Without waiting for their response, I scurry to the bathroom and lock the door once I get inside. The strong smell of bleach and other cleaning products infiltrates my nose.

At least it's clean.

I unlock my phone and call Cece.

"Need rescuing?" she asks the moment she answers the line.

"They invited my ex, and he's acting as if nothing happened. Like we're still together when I broke up with him because he made a bet with his stupid team."

"Ouch," I hear Declan faintly in the background.

"Am I on speaker?"

"Sorry," she apologizes. "It's off now. I didn't think you were going to blurt out your life story."

"Whatever. It doesn't matter." My feet move nonstop in a circle, pacing around the bathroom.

"Just tell them you have to leave. Your roommate has an emergency."

If I did that… "Jay's going to offer to drive me back and I don't want that. At all."

"Okay," she pauses for a brief moment. The phone muffles, like she placed her hand on it or something before her voice becomes clear again. "Where are you?"

"Olivewood Grill," I say.

"Tell her we'll be there in ten minutes," Declan calls out from the background.

"We?"

She hums. "As if he'd let me be around you know who."

My father. Right.

"Okay, ten minutes. I'll see you then."

The call ends and I take a deep breath.

I can handle ten minutes, right?

FIVE MINUTES GO by and I'm still in the bathroom. People are going to think I'm taking a shit, but the less time I am at the table with Jay, the better.

A soft knock comes to the door, and my attention immediately darts over to it. "Occupied."

"Sweetheart, are you okay in there?" my mother asks from the other side.

No. "Yes."

"Are you sure you don't need any help? I know it's hard for you to—"

"I'm fine, mom!" I call out before she embarrasses me because it's not hard for me to clean myself, not anymore. Not since I was in middle school.

"Ok. Jay is talking to your father," she tells me. "Apparently you never told him you were serious about leaving the school."

"Everyone, who needed to know, knew."

"But Jay's your boyfriend. He should have been the first person you told. I thought you loved him."

It could have been a possibility if he hadn't accepted that bet. If I hadn't overheard him talking about making a bet with his friends. If I hadn't witnessed him cheating on me!

"Is something going on between you two?"

There's no way I want to be trapped and have this

conversation. I glance around the bathroom. A small window a foot or two higher than me is the only escape route.

Aria could climb on the sink, reach, and pull herself through. But I don't have that kind of upper body strength. My only escape is through that door and to face the obstacle on the other side: My mother.

Be brave, be bold, be ballsy.

I walk over to the door and take a deep breath. My hand turns the nob. Opening it just a crack, I glance at my mother's worried face. "We broke up."

My mother blinks twice. Her mouth parts and she throws her arms over me. "Oh sweetheart, why didn't you tell us? We wouldn't have invited him if we knew."

She pulls us apart and looks over me like she's making sure I'm not hurt or haven't been crying. She furrows her eyebrows, confused. "But then why would he—oh maybe he wants you back. Realized he made a terrible mistake letting you go."

My mother drags me back to the table, spouting possibilities. I tune her out. There's no point in listening when I know none of what she's saying could ever be true.

I open my mouth to tell her, but we reach the table. My father stands and pulls my mother's seat out for her. Jay does the same and turns in our direction with a smile on his face. He never really does things like this. The only times are when we're around my parents.

Red flag, Melody.

Emotions can be blinding.

My father furrows his eyebrows at something behind us. He takes my mother's hand and holds her around the table to be seated, but he doesn't sit back down. Curiosity gets the better of me and I turn.

My shoulders drop from my ears. Relief floods through me. Declan stands by the host. I know it's him by the hat and basketball under his arm. As if he feels us staring, he glances our way and smiles. He says something to the host and then jogs in our direction.

"Oh, hey, Melody. Didn't know I'd see you here." He smiles before looking around the table. "Mr. Watson. I hope I'm not interrupting."

"No," my mother chimes in, "not at all. And you are?"

"Sorry. Sometimes I forget my manners." He reaches over the table, holding his hand out to my mother. "Declan Valencia."

"He's our star basketball player," my father announces.

"Oh, an athlete. How do you know our sweet Melody?" My mother has her eyes on Declan. She likes him already and I'm sure it's mainly because he's athletic.

"We met six months ago when I checked out the school that day." I jump in hoping it will suffice.

"So, you're friends?" my mother asks with a smirk.

Declan's arm wraps around my shoulder. "Yeah, unless she changes her mind about going on a date with me."

"She's taken," Jay speaks up from beside me. His fingers curl over the chair he still holds out.

"That's not what I heard," Declan says. "Melody told me you broke up."

"Is that true Melody?" My father glances from Declan to Jay, then me. I nod, unable to say anything. "Why didn't you tell us?"

"Honey, maybe she was embarrassed or hurt to say anything," my mother tries to ease the drama unfolding.

"With all due respect, Mr. and Mrs. Watson, this is

awkward and I'm sure it is for Melody too," Declan, for my sake, interjects.

My parents look at me, both sharing the same pained, sorrowful look in their eyes.

"I still love you, Mel," Jay blurts out. "I made a mistake and I want to make it right." My parents seem relieved by his statement; my father more so than my mother.

I shake my head, not wanting to deal with this anymore. He's lying and they can't see past their adoration for him to realize it. "This is too much. I need to go."

"I'm heading back to campus if you want a ride," Declan offers.

"But Melody, you hardly ate." My father points to my plate. Still full, just a few bites were taken out of the pasta.

"At least take it to go." My mother takes hold of my father's hand for support.

"I'm not really hungry."

"Don't worry, I'll make sure she gets some food on campus."

A soft smile forms on my mother's face. "Thank you, Declan was it?"

"Yes, Declan Valencia."

"It's nice to know our daughter has a caring and supportive friend on campus."

"Of course," he bows his head, "I'll see you around campus, Mr. Watson."

"A pleasure as always," my father mutters.

Declan squeezes my shoulder. Without another word to my parents or Jay, for that matter, I follow Declan out of the restaurant. The cold autumn breeze nips at my cheeks, placing an icy kiss against them.

"He looks like a prick."

"That's because he is," I say, noting the mirrored version of the man beside me. Cassius leans against a black Jeep, hands in his pockets. He lifts his head and his gaze drifts to me.

Why is he here?

"Where's Cece?" I ask a moment too soon. Cece pops her head out of the window just as I finish the question.

"I brought you a rescue crew. Figured Declan could get you out of there as quickly as possible."

"I would have been quicker if her dick of an ex didn't try to stake his claim." Declan rounds the car with a smirk.

"What did he do?" Cass asks with an edge in his tone.

"Chill, he only said she was taken." Declan laughs. "But *our girl* Melody is strong."

As if. I could barely speak for most of the time we were there.

I am weak.

A sigh leaves my lips and I walk to the car door. "Let's just go. I'm tired."

Cass opens the door. My gaze catches his, full of worry. Almost like he can see I'm more exhausted and emotionally drained than anything. I thank him as I climb in next to Cece.

"Anytime," Cass says as he gently closes the door.

Cece's arm comes around me, and I lean into her for comfort.

"Anytime, love," she whispers against my hair.

And for once, I believe it.

For once, I have people I can truly count on.

17

DECENT-SIZED MAN

CASSIUS

After last night, all I want is to make Melody smile.

The defeated look on her face is stuck in my head. Those moonlight eyes lacked their usual shimmer, and her gaze stayed glued to the floor the entire way home. She didn't even say anything, just walked into her room and allowed the darkness to consume her.

But today is a new day.

And I'll be damned if I let her sulk for another second.

I plan to make her pancakes. The problem is, I have no idea what her favorite is, if she even likes them, or if she has any allergies.

I shake my head and head for the cupboard. I open it and reach for the flour. She shouldn't be allergic to flour—not when she once made this apartment smell like a bakery.

I set the bag on the counter, but the seams snap open, and white powder spills onto the countertop and floors.

"Fuck me," I grumble.

The sound of Melody's door opening grabs my attention. She stands there, her eyes on me and the mess I made in our kitchen. A small smile comes to her face.

Thank fuck.

My insides melt, glad that it's the first thing I'm able to see this morning. She's in a pair of black sweats, and a matching hoodie. Her hair is tied in a mess of a bun. She walks over toward me but keeps to the other side of the counter.

"Were you trying to make yourself sweet?" she asks, giggling.

A chuckle leaves my lips. Everything about her is contagious; that laugh, her smile. She can infect me all she wants. "Flour isn't really sweet."

"No," she places a finger on her cheek, "but adding vanilla, chocolate chips, and a lot of sugar can change that."

I narrow my eyes at her as she moves around the counter and makes her way to the cabinets. "You'd rather have cookies than pancakes for breakfast?"

"Cookies are good for any time of the day. This belly doesn't discriminate."

My gaze drifts down to her stomach, hiding behind that black hoodie. "What belly? You hardly have any meat there."

"How would you know?" she asks.

I raise an eyebrow at her, giving her a chance to back down or at least realize *I do know.* Her eyebrows draw together and she shakes her head. "That was a long time ago."

"Six months isn't that long."

"What were you trying to make?" she asks, clearly changing the subject.

"Pancakes. Or at least, I thought about it and then realized I didn't know what you'd like or if you have any allergies."

She turns her back to me and opens the cabinets. Climbing on her tippy toes, she tries to look deeper in. Not that it matters. Melody is still too short to really see anything behind what's front and center.

"What're you looking for?"

"Another thing of flour." Melody looks around the kitchen and then walks over to the wooden table. She grabs a chair, dragging it over to the counter like she doesn't have a decent-sized man around to help her so she doesn't get hurt.

I move closer to her, placing my hand on the chair before she can hop on. "Let me look for it."

"You know I do this all the time right?"

Our gazes meet. She tilts her head, waiting for me to let go so she can go on. But there's no way in hell I'll let her. I push the chair away and reach through the cabinet for another bag of flour. And *not* to my surprise, there is none.

"Pancakes and cookies are out of the question."

She sighs, her shoulders slumping. *Damn, she really wanted those cookies.*

"We're still going to the store, right?" I ask. "We can get some more flour and a small ladder."

She opens her mouth like she's about to protest, but I'm not about to let her endanger herself with a flimsy chair. It might be fine to sit on, but the legs wobble. It's not safe, and I'd rather get something that will keep her from falling.

"It's sturdier than a chair," I add.

Melody bites her bottom lip. Her gaze falls to the floor, fingers fidgeting. "Okay, fine but we're getting food on the way there."

"Anything specific?" I ask as I lift the chair and bring it back to its original spot. "House of Pancakes, Redwood Diner, Bagel shop, or the coffee shop down the street?"

"Diner. They have those Belgian waffles with fruit."

Perfect, I haven't been there in forever.

"You might want to clean up first though," Melody says, pointing her finger at the counter and then waving it up and down my body.

Right. The flour.

An idea pops into my head and a smirk forms on my face.

"I should." I grab a handful of flour from the counter. "or..."

She backs away, narrowing her eyes at me. "Don't you even dare."

Reaching for her, I gently grab her waist and pull her into my chest. My other hand smears flour over her cheek. "At least it isn't in your hair."

"You're right." She grabs a handful from the counter and tosses it. Flour sprinkles over my head and hers. Her head tilts back. Melody closes her eyes, smiling up as the flour falls around us. Her sweet laughter is music to my ears. "It's like winter."

My arm tightens around her, flushing our bodies together. She molds perfectly into me like we're two halves of a whole. Melody looks at me. Her beautiful moonlit eyes have that sparkle back in them. Her cheeks flush a shade of pink and her tongue darts out, tracing over those plump pouty lips of hers.

I can feel her heartbeat against mine. Or maybe that's just my own, beating for the both of us. My thumb brushes over her cheek, wiping the white substance off.

I breathe her lavender scent in. She has sunspots trickling over the arch of her nose, and I keep my gaze on that, afraid to look anywhere else.

"Cass?" she whispers. I'm drawn to her eyes as they flicker down to my mouth.

Shit.

When she says my name like *that* it's hard not to pick her up and place her on the counter. I close my eyes and take a deep breath.

She's your roommate, Cass. You can't do this.

The hell I can't. I've done it before and she loved every second.

But that was just one time.

The fact of the matter is she's my roommate. If I cave in now… I'll only cause complications for both of us.

I press my forehead to hers and breathe out. "We should both get ready, now that we're covered."

I bite down on my inner cheek, dropping my arm from her. The distance between us grows as I take a step back. I can't open my eyes, not yet… not when I can feel her gaze on me.

"You go get ready. I'll clean up first."

Her words have me opening my eyes. She's already down on her knees, pushing the flour together with her hands.

Is she serious?

"It's not your mess to clean. There's a broom in the closet. Grab it for me and I'll sweep this up." She's hesitant but does as I ask anyway. I feel like I should explain myself so I don't waste any more time. "You have more hair than I do. It's going to take you a while to get all the flour out of there."

The moment she returns with the broom, she hands it to me. Our fingers brush against one another. Our gazes meet. And I swear she takes a drop of oxygen from my lungs every time.

Melody retracts her hand first, turns, and heads off to Cece's old room, which is now hers, with the master bathroom. "I won't take too long."

"Take all the time you need," I say loud enough so she can hear me, "I'm not going anywhere."

18

HUGE PACKAGE

MELODY

Cassius steps into the kitchen with nothing but a towel wrapped around his waist. Water drips down the ends of his hair and onto his forehead. My gaze trails over the droplets decorating his body.

The tattoo across his chest paints an image of what his insides look like if someone scratches it open. White inked ribs hold pink lungs and an anatomical heart in place. It's beautiful and sad at the same time.

It's like he's saying even though he opens himself up, his heart is still caged, keeping him safe.

I'm so screwed.

My gaze travels farther to the inked bones starting at his side and follows over the shadow grooves running down his hip bone and under the—

"You need to stop looking at me like that," he gruffs out.

My attention snaps right up to his face as he walks toward me. The counter is our barrier. His hip presses against it.

I want to run my tongue over every part and dry him off.

No. No. No.

"Wh-what do you mean?" I ask, feeling the heat rush to my face.

He leans forward. The counter seems so small now that his face is nearly inches from mine. His scent; vanilla and sugar, has my mouth watering. Not only does he look delicious, but he smells it too.

My inner voice is screeching right now. I can't. He's just this *huge* package of hotness. And that's not including his dick.

Oh fuck.

His mouth closes, and it's only now that I realize he's talking. "Wait, what?" I manage to let out.

He wets his lips, and I let out a shaky breath.

"I said, you're looking at me like a hungry animal."

I mean, he's not wrong. I am starving… just not for food anymore. My body is craving a sweet tattoo artist covered in ink.

As if he'll ever desire me just as badly.

The negative thought seeps through my chest, making it heavy. I try to counter it. But after earlier, part of me believes it. He would have kissed me if that wasn't the case.

Anyone else would have.

"Hey," he calls to me and I'm brought out of my head. Back to this moment. His eyes are on me, soft and worried. His cool touch brushes against my cheek. "You disappeared for a second there."

"I'm sorry," I say, taking a step back. His hand drops from my face. "Everything is cleaned up more now."

Cass trails his gaze over me. My arms instinctively wrap around my chest. "Everything but you."

I furrow my eyebrows and glance down. My hoodie and sweatpants are covered in flour after I already showered. "I'll get ready now."

Rounding the counter, I keep my gaze cast downward and try to pass him, but he steps in my way. My eyes catch the inked bones again.

What do people call those again?

"Cumgutters?" My mouth widens as I hear those words leave my thoughts and slip from my tongue.

I can feel his gaze on the top of my head. A chuckle escapes him "What did you just say?"

Shit, he heard me. It's okay. It's okay. I try to ignore the sudden heat flaring through my body. I need to leave. Get away from him and this kitchen and his wet body. But he's expecting a response and I know if I leave, I'll avoid him all day and we'll never go to the store.

And I really want to go.

Be brave, be bold, be ballsy.

Be brave, be bold, be ballsy.

Be brave, be bold, be ballsy.

"Cumgutters," I say slowly, trying to channel my inner Aria. Reaching out, my fingers graze the inked bones on his skin. He shivers at my touch and I glance up. "That's what people call them, right?"

His Adam's apple bobs as he swallows. Warm fingers cover mine. His hooded sunlight eyes stare back at me, pleading.

"Don't do that, moonlight," he whispers, "it was hard enough to get rid of your phantom touches the first time. I've yet to erase the ones from the other night."

My heart races to the same beat as the wings fluttering in my stomach. He draws me in like Icarus. If I'm not careful, I'll burn to a crisp and fall too hard into a pit of despair.

Fear crawls through the depths of my brain. There are plenty of reasons why I shouldn't dive into anything with Cassius.

Our moment was a one-time thing.

My dad doesn't like him.

He withheld the truth and let me think Declan was sunlight for an entire week.

Jay also started out nice. How can I expect Cassius won't be the same?

Yet none of that stops my mouth from responding, "I haven't forgotten yours."

But you did forget him.

A war brews within those sunlight eyes of his, fire and ice battling it out. I'm not sure which is winning or if I should even be rooting for one over the other. Fire maybe? Unless that means destruction.

Maybe we shouldn't have thrown ourselves into this kind of trouble. If only he didn't come out with just a—my gaze drops from his and lands right down to his—

"Go get ready," he says, stealing my attention away from the tent under his towel. He takes a step back, letting his hand fall from mine. "Before we both do something we shouldn't."

But why shouldn't we? I want to ask, but he turns his heels and heads for his room.

"Just do me a favor," he calls out, "don't make my mistake and walk out in just a towel."

I furrow my eyebrows, letting curiosity fall from my lips. "Why not?"

His footsteps stop and I walk over, just to see him turn his head in my direction. "Because I won't be able to control myself and you'll end up right on top of that counter, legs wrapped around my head as I taste every last inch of you."

He leaves me there in the hall. My mouth agape. Cheeks flared.

If I wasn't craving his touch before, I definitely am now.

136

19

MY TASTES HAVE CHANGED

CASSIUS

All it takes is one step into the diner to remember why I haven't been here in forever.

Straight brown hair and an hourglass figure catch my attention. She's turned from us, but I know those hips anywhere. I pray I'm wrong. However, the moment she shifts to take the menu from the host, and that dimpled smile is revealed, I know my prayer isn't answered.

Her gaze lands on Melody and then drifts to me. She halts. Those green eyes are soft, a reminder that looks are deceiving.

"Cassius." She might be smiling, but those eyes are trying to penetrate my soul. Pretty faces and sweet smiles are dangerous.

Especially on Cara.

"And here I thought you were avoiding this place because of me."

"Nope," I say, ignoring her flirtatious tone. "Just been busy with work."

I look at Melody and place my hand on the small of her back, making sure she doesn't get left behind.

Cara leads us to *our* old booth and places the menus down. "You always were a busy man. Do you need some time or do you just want the usual?"

She hasn't taken a second glance at Melody. It's like she's purposely ignoring her. My jaw tics at the thought.

My gaze drifts to Melody who seems to be lost in her own world. My finger taps against her back and that seems to do the trick. She looks up at me, then at the booth.

Melody presses her hand on the table and slides in. Unable to get to the other side, without having to pass or ask Cara to move, I climb in beside Melody. I slide a menu between us. "Do you want to look at the menu first?"

Melody shakes her head. "I know what I want."

I nod, watching as her pouty lips part. She orders a Belgian waffle topped with strawberries and an apple juice on the side. The moment she's done I look at Cara. Her head is tilted to the side, waiting.

"Make that two." I shrug, noting her furrowed eyebrows. "My tastes have changed."

"Noted." Cara smiles and, thankfully, walks away.

Now that she's gone, I move into the space across the table. "Sorry about that."

"About what?" Melody asks, drifting her attention from the window.

"Our waitress."

"Why?" she asks, worry swirling in her eyes. "What happened?"

I tilt my head, raising an eyebrow. "You really weren't paying attention?"

"I was kind of focused on Aria dragging Sergio to a small

diner then I thought it wouldn't happen because they're both rich." She shrugs. Her finger draws little circles into the table. "But I have this scene for the future when they're on the run, hiding from her betrothed in a hotel and they can go to a diner next to that."

A smile tugs on the corner of my mouth. Most people would just say no and carry on with their day. Instead, Melody tells stories. She weaves these ideas and brings them together. Masterpieces I'm sure, but I've yet to read what she's written.

"Did she say something?" Melody asks.

I shake my head. "No. She's just not someone you should worry about."

"Two apple juices," Cara announces her return and places both glasses in the middle of the table.

I keep my gaze on Melody who has hers on Cara. She seems fascinated, taking in every detail of Cara's face.

They didn't name her Carabella for nothing.

But she's not a natural beauty. She has a painted pink smile and a face clear of any blemishes, mostly, due to makeup. Her eyelashes are long, but also fake and her long brown hair looks better without the assistance of heating tools.

I don't need to look at her to know all of this. Seeing her brings the memories front and center.

All of our study sessions in her dorm. The library where we had our first kiss. The way she'd purposely stain my neck with her lipstick, marking me as hers. The late nights we shared talking about life and our plans after college. The arguments turned into screaming sessions.

Her slapping me in the face, then claiming my fingerprints on her neck were from abuse when the truth was she asked me to wrap my hand around her neck and fuck her. Her constantly flirting around. The jealousy she held even when she was the only woman I saw. The night she declared we go on a break, just so she could fuck some basketball players. Then, of course, the final straw was when she had the nerve to talk badly about both of my siblings before giving me an ultimatum:

It's me or this place. It can't be both.

But her speaking about my siblings in a negative light cemented my choice.

And I'd do it again, no matter who it is.

"So how've you been Cass?" she asks, sliding into the booth right beside me.

"I'm doing fine. Shouldn't you be working?"

"You're here." Her shoulder brushes against mine. "I might as well catch up with an old friend."

"We're not friends, Cara and it's really disgusting that you'd try to get close to me when I'm clearly with someone right now."

"Oh, you two are together?" Cara asks. I can hear the disappointment in her voice as she slowly steps out of the booth. "I didn't know."

"Yes," I say before Melody can even think of saying otherwise. "We are."

"Guess your tastes *have* changed." Her attitude grabs my attention. Her focus is on Melody. She gives a curt smile and shrugs. "I'll go check on your food."

She walks away and I let out the biggest sigh. My fingers run through my hair. "I'm sorry about all of this."

Melody looks to where Cara walked off and then back at me. "She really likes you. Why did you tell her we were together?"

"Let me ask you something," I grab my drink and pull it closer to my side. "Would you want your ex around you?"

Melody blinks twice, lowering her head. She places both hands around her drink and taps her fingers against the glass. "You used to date her?"

"Shocking, I know. A guy like me dating someone like her." I pick up my drink and take a sip.

"Why's that shocking? You're both hot."

A smirk forms on my lips. "Hot, huh?"

"Oh come on, don't act like you don't know this. You and your brother look exactly alike," she says as if I see my brother as attractive. "The only difference is he walks around flirting and you don't."

"So let me get this straight. You think my ex is hot, which, I can admit she is. But she's definitely not who I thought she was and…" I continue with a smirk on my face. "You find my brother hot."

"And your sister. And Olivia, I think her name was?"

"Ophelia," I correct, knowing my brother's best friend would stab me with a pen if I didn't. "So everyone around me is hot which means that includes you."

She laughs. "No."

"No?" I straighten up, crossing my arms. "Right, you think you're nothing."

"I am nothing."

"We gotta work on that self-esteem," I mutter.

"What?" she asks, leaning into the booth. "It's true. I'm not."

"You're my roommate. A friend, at least to me. You're a student; someone's daughter and sister. Interesting, funny, open-minded, caring, and creative. Beautiful, which in my opinion is better than hot."

Melody scoffs. She rolls up her sleeves, exposing her scars, and stretches her arms across the table. "You call this beautiful? It makes people stare."

I hate the way she keeps putting herself down. She doesn't see her worth, her beauty and it fucking kills me. But I hold down the anger brewing in my chest and the sadness drowning my lungs. "People stare at all kinds of things, Melody. They even stare at my tattoos."

"Because they're beautiful and tell a story."

I reach out and place my hands under hers. Moonlight eyes stare back at me, ready to burst into tears. She's breaking my heart, and she hasn't even claimed it.

"But that's exactly what I see when I look at you." My voice is soft, only for her ears. "There's a story among those scars. Good or bad, a mixture of both... it's there, Melody and if people can't see beyond that, they aren't worth your fucking time."

A lone tear breaks free, but she quickly wipes it away with the back of her hand.

"I think you're beautiful, hot, sexy, and smart. There's a lot of pain and self-hatred in there too, I can see it. And even though I'm just getting to know you, I've enjoyed every second of it." Reaching over the table, I brush a second tear leaving her eyes. "Even when I hate seeing you like this, I still enjoy getting to know all of you."

Cara clicks her heels loud enough in our direction to break our moment. Melody lowers my hand from her face, and I take the opportunity to slide my fingers between hers. Her hand is small, much smaller compared to mine. It's the size of a toddler's. I can't help but wonder if the surgeries had anything to do with the growth stunt.

Cara places our plate in front of us as Melody looks at her

with a smile. No one says another word. Cara leaves to tend to her tables and Melody slips her hand from mine.

As much as I don't want her to, I let her crawl back into her space.

"I like you, Melody," I say as she digs her fork and knife into the waffle.

Liking her is an understatement. There's definitely more to it. Something grows in the depths of my chest, sprouting, and trying to make a home. Whatever it is, I know it has something to do with Melody. It's always there, squirming when she's around. Even if I can't be with her, I can at least admit that.

Melody sighs, drifting her attention to me. "My ex pretended to have feelings for me so he could win a bet."

That wasn't the response I was expecting. It's also one that rubs me the wrong way. "Are you fucking serious? Why the hell was he at dinner with your parents then?"

"I don't know." She shakes her head, dropping her fork on the plate. "I really have no idea what he wants. He said he loves me."

"Bullshit," I grunt.

"I know. It's just… I want you to understand it's not that I don't believe you. I just…"

"You don't trust me," I say. "It's fine. Your reasons are valid." I grab my fork, break a piece of my waffle, and hold it out to her lips. "She didn't have good things to say about Deck or Cece. Told me to choose the tattoo shop or her."

"That's not fair."

I shake my head. It wasn't but it gave me the clarity I needed to cut all ties with her. "Eat, Melody."

She looks down at the piece, then back to me. Leaning in slowly, she parts her lips and takes the bite. She chews, closing her eyes as if to savor the taste. "It's a shame we can't come here anymore."

Laughter escapes from the depths of my chest. "We can find somewhere better. Hurry up and eat so we can get out of here."

A smile forms on Melody's face, brightening up the shit mood I seemed to have put us both in for a while.

She once called me sunlight and I understand why. The sun burns and brings the worst to light. But Melody is like the moonlight, carefully moving in, illuminating the best even in the dark.

And I can't seem to keep myself from smiling at her in return.

Yeah, I definitely chose the right name for her.

20

DEFINITELY NOT DADDY

MELODY

Cassius likes me.

My heart flutters at the thought and those sunlight eyes bring warmth, comfort, and happiness—something I haven't felt in a long time.

I hum, walking down the snack aisle. My hand grips the cart, dragging it behind me. People pass by and stare, but I don't care. I'm having a good time and nothing will stop that.

My gaze rises to the top shelf across from us. A large plastic bear container stuffed with animal crackers sits staring at me. *Yes. Absolutely, yes.*

I walk over and tilt my head, assessing the height. *I could grab it.* My foot kicks an item from the bottom shelf in, and I climb. My hand tries to grab it, fingers try to move it an inch so it'll be easier, but it only moves farther back.

"Again," Cass's voice grabs my attention. I don't turn back. Not when his body heat presses up against me. He reaches over and pushes the container of animal crackers off the edge so it falls into my arms. "Just ask me to get it for you."

"But you saw me looking at it."

"There's plenty of snacks to look at." His hand slides over my hips as he spins me and our gazes meet. "How can I know what you want if you don't tell me?"

I want you.

My tongue darts out, wetting my lips. He tries to pull me close, but the plastic container keeps us at a distance. "I'll tell you next time."

He shakes his head and smiles. Taking a step back, he gives me more space.

My arms wrap around the bear's neck so it doesn't fall. "I feel like a little kid."

Cass chuckles. His gaze travels down and back up my body. "You look like a little kid who won't let go of the toy their parent refuses to buy."

"Does that mean you're not buying this for me, *Daddy*?"

He rolls his eyes. "If you call me daddy again, not at all."

I chuckle. "Got it."

"You're lucky no one is in this aisle," he says as he reaches the cart. His hand flexes over the handle. "That'd be really awkward."

I shrug, not bothering to put the animal crackers in the cart. Not that there's any room for it. "I guess. Sergio doesn't like being called daddy either, I think. Aria's never called him that."

"What about you?" he asks, and I turn my attention to Cass. He leans over the cart, eyes glued to me.

"Me?"

"Yeah." He smirks, tilting his head. "What does Melody like being called?"

I blink twice. He already knows… that look in his eyes tells me he does. "Definitely not daddy."

A laugh bursts from his lips laughs and he shakes his head. He pushes the cart forward, ready to go but one of the boxes is knocked off. Cassius looks over, stops the cart, and walks around, picking up the Beast figurine I chose for my bookcase. "You know, I wasn't expecting to have a full cart when I said we could come here."

"Always prepare to get more. We come here for one thing and leave with the entire store."

"I mean, you're not wrong." He tosses the box into the cart and pulls it along with us as we head for the next aisle. "I just hope you weren't assuming this was going to take us all day."

"Why?" I ask, fixing the bear container in my arms as we walk side by side.

"Because you asked to spend all day together."

Oh. Right. I hadn't entirely thought our day through. Breakfast and the store were the only two things I really thought about. And possibly dinner. Maybe lunch. Besides, I still have to read and make notes for class. "What if we just spend it at home? We can do our schoolwork together or something."

"Will you be cooking dinner?" he asks, glancing over, "Since you canceled on me last night."

I smile, nodding. "Yeah. I can cook us dinner. What do you want to eat?"

"Surprise me."

That doesn't help at all. I can't surprise him when I don't even know what he likes to eat. "Are you allergic to anything?"

He shrugs. "As far as I know, no. Not a big fan of fish."

Good. Neither am I. "Italian? I can make a Capers salad, some stuffed shells, Alfredo, Chicken Parm, Malfatti…"

"What?"

"They're these spinach ricotta dumplings."

Cass groans, placing his hand over his stomach. "See now you're just making me hungry."

"I promise you'll be satisfied by the end of the night." My arm tightens around the bear in my arms and I turn, the moment I don't hear the cart beside me. "What?"

Cass shakes his head. "I'm just surprised you didn't try to apologize."

I tilt my head. All I said was his stomach would be satisfied. "For what?"

He shakes his head and smirks, pushing the cart again. "Nothing, Moonlight."

I shrug and keep looking around the store. From the food aisle to the make-up section. The area is packed with other women testing out lipsticks on their hands. Luckily, I don't need to go down there, but Cass stops and glances over.

"I'll wait here if you want to go."

Scrunching my face up, I shake my head. "I'm good. I don't really wear much."

Only on special occasions like dates, family outings or dinners, orientation, my first day at the new school, and shopping trips with my hot roommate. Those kinds of things.

"I know. I've only seen you wear it once."

"It's only for special occasions." I shrug with a smirk.

"Then we're going to have to make some." Cass reaches over, sliding his arm around my shoulder. "Is it okay if I hold you like this?"

My eyes widen, and my cheeks are suddenly hot. I nod, unable to say what I really want.

You can touch me anyway. Any place. Any time.

"Good because I like it when you're close."

"You swear this isn't some joke?" *Fuck my internal negative thoughts for blurting out.*

Cass stares at me for a moment. He lets go of the cart and places his other hand on my shoulder. His forehead dips until it rests against mine. "Am I going to have to prove that to you too?"

"I-I don't know."

"I would never play a cruel joke like that on anyone. Leading you on is the last thing I'd want to do. I said I like you because I wanted you to know. That doesn't mean I'm falling head over heels for you," he says, "You don't have to feel pressured. You don't have to worry about me overstepping boundaries. We're roommates. Friends. And if one day you start to feel more than that I want you to feel comfortable enough to tell me instead of hiding away."

No. This definitely is a joke. It has to be. No one ever said such romantic or nice words to another person.

Taking a step back, I swallow the lump in my throat. "I don't trust you."

"That's ok. Trust is earned. One day you'll see there's no ulterior motive and maybe when you do, I'll be able to have some more answers for you about how I feel."

If they don't disappear before then.

21

INKED HEARTS

CASSIUS

Once I told Melody I liked her, there was no going back. And maybe that's selfish of me, but what's done is done. Yet, I still can't ignore this itching need to get closer to her. It's an issue which is why I had to get out of the house.

I push the door to Inked Hearts open. The bell above rings, announcing my arrival, but no one seems to notice.

The first person to catch my eye is Declan. He sits by the wall, his feet propped on the portable heater we got for the winter. His eyes focus on the orange ball spinning on his finger. He doesn't have a care in the world and doesn't even look in my direction.

And why would he?

He knows it's me.

Cece, on the other hand, lifts her gaze from her phone as she sits behind the front desk. Her manicured blue nails tap on her phone, texting away without looking.

I swear Cece's secretly superhuman.

She raises her eyebrow like she's waiting for me to tell her something. Like she knows I have something to get off my chest.

"I have a problem." My siblings don't make any moves or sound to my announcement, so I continue. "It's about Melody."

Cece's lips curve into a smile. She pushes her seat in and flips her phone face down on the desk. Declan's ball drops from his finger onto his lap and I know he's listening too.

Nerves suddenly prick at my skin. They're both waiting and I have no idea how to get this out without them trying to push it into more than what it can be.

"I," a sigh leaves my lips and my fingers run through my hair, "told Melody I like her."

"Because *that* wasn't obvious." Declan tosses his ball in the air, catching it when it comes back down. "You two dating now?"

A scoff leaves my lips as I roll my eyes. He knows more than anyone that's not a reason to dive into dating. "No. I don't have time to."

"Then make time," Cece jumps in, placing her elbows on the armrest. "How long has it been since you were actually interested in someone?"

If I exclude that one night with Melody and the disastrous date with whatshername, it's been about a year or so. I can't even remember when Cara and I made our breakup official.

"Cass." My sister calls for my attention, her voice soft. "You like someone. They like you. That's a win. Take the chance and just go for it. Don't be Deck."

"Yeah don't be—hey. Ophie deserves someone better than me."

"I'm not starting this argument with you again. Cass..." Cece turns her attention back to me. "Just ask her out on a date. One date won't kill you. You can decide on a relationship later."

"Most people just assume you're in a relationship when you're dating." Declan shrugs.

And that's partially the problem. The weight on my shoulder drops and I glance over realizing I still have my backpack on. I move to the side and take a seat, still by the door. My backpack falls from my shoulder to the floor with a light thud. "I don't want to make things complicated."

"You made it complicated when you fell on your ass for her six months ago," Declan scoffs, turning toward me. He raises his eyebrow, a silent dare for me to deny the truth. "Or you can just fuck her and get it over with."

"I'm not doing that," I tell him.

"Technically you already did," Cece chimes in.

A door in the back crashes against the wall as it opens. Footsteps slap on the wooden floors and Maverick's figure comes into view.

"I'm so sick of hearing about your issues, Cass." He leans against the wall, crossing his arms. Green eyes narrow in my direction. "She's single, you're single. She's not your best friend, your cousin's ex, your sibling's friend, or your best friend's girlfriend."

Both of my siblings lower their heads. I try not to look in Cece's direction as I wonder which one of Maverick's accusations belongs to her. Declan and his are obvious, but Cece's... not so much.

"Let me ask you something," Maverick drags my attention back to him, "have you ever thought about asking what *she* wants instead of just assuming she'll want to date you or be in a relationship?"

The sudden question stabs me right in the gut. Maverick's lectures are like a knife, sharp and precise.

Why would she want to date me?

"You're right," I say, nodding my head—my heart suddenly feeling heavy. My gaze drifts back up to him, though I'm unsure as to when it actually fell. "I should ask. Not every person is looking for something serious."

Even if she does deserve to have someone who's devoted to her.

"You've been off your shit lately." Maverick sighs and his gaze softens. His own silent apology, not that he has to. I needed to hear him say it. "Stop thinking so much about this. She's your roommate. Whatever happens, happens."

"Is that what you tell yourself with Xy?" Declan chimes in with a chuckle. A horrible mistake on his part. I glance over, hoping he'll keep his mouth shut, but the damage has been done.

"No, I tell myself the same thing I tell *my* ex: Don't even bother."

Declan stares at Maverick, unfazed by his words. I'm sure it's because Declan tries to tell Ophelia the same. "Too bad she's yet to listen."

"Alright, enough." Cece stands from her seat. Her hands slam against the desk. "Declan, that's a low blow. Mave, seriously? And Cass."

My shoulders drop, just as the sternness in her voice does. "Yeah?"

"You have one client for the day, coming in an hour. You're free after, so take the time to just relax. Go draw or something. The answers will come to you."

They might not.

Still, I take her words with me as I inch my way toward my station. Carefully, I pass Maverick. His anger radiates off his body with his gaze is still focused on Declan. I have a feeling they're going to go at it, more than likely in private—away from Cece. I just hope neither of them ends up with bruised fists.

My name is carved into the wooden door decorated with gray dragons, hearts, ink blotches, and tattoo guns, and a moon is painted just above. It's a beacon of light for others to read whose room this is.

I push the door open, step inside, and kick it closed. The little chatter dies out and I'm left in a world of silence. No family, work, or school.

Just me.

"HEY, CASS?" Cece calls for me as a warning before the door cracks open. I stop my movements and place the pencil in my mouth, letting her know I'm listening. "Your client is here."

Pushing my chair away from my desk and drawing, I stand ready to grab them from the waiting room, but my sister moves back and my doorway is suddenly filled by a man I've barely crossed paths with.

"Surprised I've never taken the time to step in here before." His gaze takes in my little office space with a raised eyebrow. "There's not a lot of traffic or wait time."

"We haven't been in business for that long," I say, holding

my hand out to the tattooing bed. "But you already knew that. So what brings you here, Mr. Watson."

"It's my job to know the businesses around town. Make sure they're appropriate considering the university just down the road."

That doesn't answer my question, but he moves into my area anyway. The air thickens, constricting my lungs. He sits down, crossing his leg over the other.

"I'll make this short, Mr. Valencia. It seems your *brothers* have become friends with my daughter."

I hold my tongue and move over to my desk. No good will come from me saying anything to this man. Not when it'll more than likely end up with me behind bars. I lean back, letting my desk give me support. My fingers curl around the edge.

He's not done, not by the way he shifts uncomfortably. "I'd like for it to stay that way and not go any farther. She doesn't need someone in her life to confuse her."

"What does this have to do with me, Mr. Watson?"

"I'd hate for your establishment to be demolished due to unfortunate circumstances," he threatens, flicking his finger into the air.

My muscles tick. Anger vibrates through me. "Are you getting a tattoo or piercing, or are you just here to waste my time? I have work to get back to."

A small chuckle leaves him. He pushes himself up from the tattoo bed and walks over to the door. His hand holds the frame open as he takes one last look around my area. "It's a shame. So much wasted talent. You could be in an art gallery making more than what this place is worth."

I scoff at his backhanded comment. Talent means nothing unless I'm having fun and enjoying what I do. Having Inked

Hearts allows me to share what I do. I get to inspire others and make people feel proud to have ink on their skin. Or, in Melody's case, make them feel beautiful.

I owe her a tattoo if she still wants it and I really hope she does.

"I'd rather keep my art accessible and affordable." I hold my head high, taking a deep breath.

Mr. Watson shakes his head and leaves without another word.

Footsteps make their way to my area and Cece pops her head in. "What did he come here for?"

"Nothing important," I tell her. "Apparently you and Deck know his daughter."

"Oh."

Reaching out, I place my hand on her shoulder and pull her close. "Listen, I don't care who you're friends with Cece. Hell, maybe it'll do her some good. But please," I place a small kiss on her forehead. "Promise me you'll be careful."

Her hands press to my chest, shoving me away. She fights the smile coming to her lips as she shakes her head. "Come on, Cass. Tell me."

"He's just a transphobic asshole who doesn't want his daughter to get *confused*. Nothing else you have to worry about."

She huffs, taking a step back. "You can lie, but I'll find out."

"And there will be nothing you can do," I tell her. "Shouldn't you be heading out?"

She hums. "I hate the hour here, then head to lunch and class days."

"You can always skip coming here."

"And leave you to miss out on the little bit of sleep you

have, no thanks." Cece flips her hair and turns. "You sure it's nothing?"

"Cece. It's fine," I reassure her. She finally leaves, letting me sink into my chair.

Regardless of whether this building stands or not, Inked Hearts will never be taken down.

I'll make sure of it.

THE BIGGEST DICK

MELODY

"Who exactly are we eating with again?" I ask, wrapping my arms around myself to keep warm. The sun above does nothing to cancel out the autumn breeze invading my hoodie.

Cece hooks her arm around mine, stealing the last bit of hope I had for warmth. She's a little more chipper than usual, which is saying something, considering she's always in a good mood. It seems like we haven't really spent time together. She's usually busy with her job and school work, but we've managed to get down a schedule to see one another and eat lunch between classes.

Cece pulls me into the dining hall. "Ophelia, Declan. Xy, my best friend, is busy studying."

Eyes land on me almost immediately and I shake off the feeling. The chatter around us doesn't counter Cece's voice much. Especially since she leans closer to me. "So how's your book coming along?"

"Which one?" I ask because I really have no idea which one

she's talking about. I have a few on hold, Sergio and Aria's, and this new one I started searching image ideas for.

"Which one? Girl." She laughs, shaking her head. "The mafia princess one."

"Oh, Aria." My pointer fingers tap against one another. "It's going. Slow. I got stuck trying to figure out how they can get closer when he doesn't want to be near her."

"They live together, they're bound to cross paths."

"It's a big house."

"Doesn't matter. Force them together. You're the author. The creator of their universe. Push them even if it's just little moments."

It's easier said than done.

Not all characters listen. They like to steer from the plot being set or even just the idea in mind for the scene. But not many people understand this.

"Speaking of people living together, how's that going?"

Aside from Cass admitting he likes me and me still thinking there's a catch? Nothing. "We get along."

"He told me you know." Cece tilts her head, giving me an *I know everything look.*

My eyes widen. Did that mean he told her about the towel incident? Luckily an arm wraps around my shoulder, preventing me from answering. Cotton candy mixed with spice enters my nostrils.

"I can't believe you're cheating on me with my brother before our first date," Declan's playful tone rings in my ear.

"It's not cheating if we aren't together," I tell him, glancing over my shoulder.

A smirk tugs at the corner of his lips. "So you *are* with Cass."

"No!" I nearly shriek. "Not because I don't want to be with

Cass. I mean." I'm stumbling over my words again. Taking a deep breath I start over. "Did he say we were?"

Declan chuckles, rubbing his hand against my shoulder. "Nah. But I'm now curious, do you want to be with my brother?"

Cece stares at me, burning holes into the right side of my face. It's like they're aiming a spotlight at me like I'm strapped to a lie detector test like if I say the wrong answer I'll be shot in the head.

"You don't have to answer him," Cece finally says. Her fingers run circles over my arm. "We already know you do."

A nervous laugh leaves my mouth. "Is it really that obvious?"

"You should ask him out." Declan shrugs. He drops his arm from my shoulder and sprints ahead of us, sliding into the seat right next to Ophelia who's waving us in her direction.

"No pressure of course," Cece adds. "But I think you really should do it. If you wait for him, it'll never happen."

"I told him I don't trust him."

"So? Trust is earned. Cass isn't your shitty ex. He's not going to be in it for anything other than your heart. But he needs a push."

I guess I can do that.

Sliding into the chair across from Ophelia, I smile as she shoves Declan's face out of hers. "Please do me a favor and date this twin instead. He needs a good girl, not just something to dip his dick in."

"My dick has been dry for years." Declan rolls his eyes.

Beside me, Cece groans. "Can we not talk about my brother's dick? I'm trying not to vomit before I eat."

I bit down on my bottom lip, containing my chuckle. Ophelia does the opposite, letting her laugh fill the table.

"Alright, fine. Are we still having Thanksgiving at Cass's? It's what? Two weeks away?"

Cece hums. "Yeah, as far as I know. Xy said she'd join us. For Mave, it depends if his parents are doing anything. Same with his sister."

"Any word on Niko?" Declan asks before he turns to me. "He's Xy's ex."

"Not sure." Cece shrugs. "I think Cass already invited him, but you know he usually goes wherever Mave goes on holidays."

"I'm assuming you'll be there too?" Ophelia asks, grabbing my attention. She twirls a piece of her blond hair.

"I didn't know you guys were doing a Thanksgiving. I'm going to be with my family. My brother's coming home from studying abroad."

"You're coming home after, right?" Cece asks. I nod, letting her continue, "We can save you some."

"What about Julien?" Ophelia glances at Declan.

"Who's Julien?" I ask, suddenly curious about someone who has the same name as my brother.

"My friend." Declan looks back at Ophelia, then Cece. "He's coming so be prepared."

Cece groans. Her arms stretch out over the table and she drops her head. "Why?"

"I take it you don't like him?" It's obvious, but I want to make sure anyway.

"Let's just say we used to compete."

"For what, who has the biggest dick?" Ophelia chuckles.

"If we go in order—" Cece starts but is interrupted.

"Don't." Ophelia shakes her head. "I already know your brothers and Mave's. I assume Cass's is the same since they're twins and I don't need to know yours or Julien's."

"We don't." Declan chimes in. "Mine's—" Ophelia covers his mouth and I let out a breath, thanking her with a look. I don't want to know anything about Declan's stuff down there. It's enough to see Cass half naked, dripping wet, with a towel wrapped around his—

"What's wrong with you?" Someone at the table asks. I'm not sure who at this point. Their voices blend as the idea of Cass's towel inching lower overpowers my brain. "Hello, earth to Melody."

"I saw Cass in a towel" I blurt out, unable to contain the words anymore.

Why would you tell them that?

The entire table bursts with laughter.

"We all have, babe. It's not a big deal," Cece says, "to us at least."

"It's really not. Especially when I've seen this one," Ophelia slaps Declan's chest, "butt naked on more than one occasion."

"Co-ed bathrooms," Declan smirks, "gotta love them."

"Oh." Cece turns to me, propping her arm on the table. She uses her hand as a chin rest. "Your dad came into our shop earlier."

"My dad? Why would he be there?"

"Not sure entirely. Probably to tell Cass to keep us away from you. But I don't think Cass even knows you're Watson's daughter."

I look over at Ophelia, the only person at the table who shouldn't know. She doesn't flinch or make any notion that she cares about this reveal. Though, I'm sure that might be due to Declan. They are close. He probably told her.

"Only Cass knows what your dad wanted. He specifically went just to talk to Cass."

But why? My dad is notorious for trying to control

everything in his path. Does he know I'm living with Cass? No... I made sure he wouldn't find out. Maybe it's just to make them not be friends with me because he doesn't like them. But I do. And that's all that should matter.

As if Declan notices my demeanor he opens his mouth, "Whatever. That shit doesn't matter. What does is if Melody here is going to ask our older brother out on a date."

"Single, older brother," Cece adds with a chuckle.

"Oh, you're going to ask him out?" Ophelia asks. "Smart move. I don't think Cass has the balls to do it. If it was years ago, maybe but definitely not now."

"Why not?"

"It's not my place to say, but I say ask him out before his ex tries to."

His ex... the beautiful woman from the diner. He'd be a fool not to agree to that.

As if anyone would really date someone like her—No.

I shake the negative thought from my head.

Someone would date me.

Cass paid more attention to me than her when we were getting food. He actually cared and wanted me to believe there was more to me than just the negative thoughts that tried to make their way out.

I had a chance...

"What's that thing you say?" Cece drags my attention to her. Her smile widens and I know exactly what she's asking me to do.

Be brave, be bold, be ballsy.

LOOK ME IN THE EYES

CASSIUS

I step out of my room, surprised to not see Melody waiting for me. I woke up a little later than usual since Declan promised to get Karaoke ready on his own. It's a setup, I'm sure, but it gives me some time to spend with Melody.

A grunt comes from her room, followed by a loud bang. Curiosity grips me, drawing me to her room. A small choke comes from the room, followed by whimpers.

"Melody?" I call out, tapping my knuckles against the door. There's a long pause before she finally answers.

"Y-yeah?" Her voice breaks, cracking a piece of my heart.

"Are you ok in there?" *Dumb question.* Clearly, she's not, but I need confirmation.

She doesn't answer. I swallow hard, tempted to turn the doorknob and let myself in. Anxiety pricks at my skin, crawling up my arm. It knows what happened the last time I didn't open. How if I'd been a minute sooner, I wouldn't have found my twin nearly dead on the bed with a bottle of pills in his hand.

"Melody," I knock once more, my voice strained, "please answer me."

The doorknob turns and the door cracks open. I peer inside, my gaze falling right on her face. Her eyes are puffy, her cheeks stained with tears, and her nose bright like a cherry.

My palm presses against the wood, opening the door fully. I step inside, invading her space. My hands cup her face. I tilt her chin up. "What's the matter?"

She sniffles, shaking her head. "I can't do my hair."

I blink twice, uncertain if I heard her correctly. "What?"

"I can't do my hair." She pulls away from me, curling into herself. "What's the point of being an adult and trying to live on your own when you can't even put your hair up in a damn ponytail?"

A smile tugs at the corner of my mouth. I shouldn't smile, shouldn't find her adorable, but I do. Fuck. She's so cute with that pouty little mouth of hers.

Unable to help myself, I pinch her bottom lip and tug playfully on it. "Is that really what has you so upset right now?"

"Yes!" she cries. Tears burst from her eyes and she chokes, trying to hold her breath.

"Moonlight, breathe." I pull her into a hug, running my hand along her spine. "It's ok. Doing a ponytail is hard."

She mumbles into my chest. Her small hands grip my shirt as she sobs. My chin rests on top of her head, letting her tears soak through the fabric. I hold her tighter. "It's ok, Melody. If you really want your hair up, I can always do it for you."

She rubs her face against me and lifts her head. I rub my thumb under her eyes, washing away the tears staining her face. Fuck, I want so badly to kiss her rosy plump lips and wipe away her troubles.

"You can?" She asks, sniffling.

"Yeah, I used to brush Cece's hair all the time when we were kids." *Before my mom made her cut it after someone stuck gum in it.* "Then we can head to Karaoke."

Her eyes widen. "Oh no, you're late aren't you?"

I chuckle softly. "It's fine. Let's get your hair done first."

"You can just put it up. I don't care if it's messy."

Spinning her around, I place my hands on her shoulder. "Got a scrunchy?"

She nods, holding her wrist up. I slide the band off of hers and onto mine. My fingers comb her hair. I try to ignore the thoughts of her bent at the waist, her soft flesh bouncing against my—I shake the image from my head and gently pick at the knots. Her hair is longer than before. Still smooth. Inhaling the scent of lavender, I grab all her hair and tie it into a ponytail.

"All set." I shift, calming down the *need* growing in my pants. "We should get going."

"Can we have dinner or go out together?" She asks as she turns to face me.

"Isn't that what we already do, eat and go out? I mean we're going out now."

Melody shakes her head, glancing down at her feet. A blush spreads across her face.

Wait... "Are you asking me out on a date?"

"If you don't want to, we don't have to, I just thought I'd ask. You know, shoot my shot. That sounds terrible coming from—"

I close the little space between us, pressing my chest to

hers. My fingers grip her chin, lifting it as I lower my face to meet hers. She's nervous and I don't want her to be. She should feel confident, *be* confident enough to ask because there's no way in hell I'd ever say no to her. "If you're going to ask me out, you should look me in the eyes while you do it."

My heart thumps, or maybe it's hers. At this point, I'm not sure. She bites down on her lower lip. And I can't help but be drawn by it. Her breath is shaking against my mouth.

"Cass, will you go on a date with me?"

My lips curl into a smile. My nose brushes gently against hers. "Right now?"

She shakes her head. "No...maybe after Thanksgiving. If you aren't busy."

"It gives me enough time to clear my schedule."

"Great." She moves back and I let my hand fall from her face, giving her the space she's not verbally asking for. She turns from me, walks over to her bed, and grabs a sweater.

"I have a follow-up question."

She spins on her heels, furrowing her eyebrows. "If you're going to ask if I like you, I think the answer is obvious."

Cute, she found her backbone.

"Actually." I have to word this correctly, so she wouldn't think I was asking her. "I was wondering if you *would ever* consider being in a relationship."

"With you?"

"No, with my brother." I roll my eyes, giving her a small smirk.

She shrugs. "He's not really my type, but you can ask me again after we go out on a date."

Melody pulls her sweater over her head and takes a step toward me. She holds her hand out and I take it, weaving my fingers between hers. My hand covers hers, but she has the power, gripping so that we stay connected.

I tug her close, cupping her cheek. Leaning down, I take the chance and place a small kiss on her forehead. A date after Thanksgiving...

I'm definitely looking forward to it.

BROKEN HEART AND A FRAGILE EGO

MELODY

If there's one place I always feel comfortable it's at my parent's house. The familiarity of the place calms me more than anything, even as the smell of turkey surrounds me the moment I step inside. I don't bother calling out to let them know I'm here. The sweet blends of a piano escaping from the speakers wouldn't let them hear, anyway.

I walk through the hall, passing the empty living room. Various paintings adorn the walls. Vases take up space in each corner. Light chatter can be heard as I get closer. I turn into the dining room where my father is sitting at the head of the table.

Julien, my brother, is the first to look in my direction. His dark gray eyes soften as his gaze lands on me. He stands, and a bright smile grows on his face. "I almost thought I'd have to come find you myself."

I chuckle as he rounds the table. His steps grow longer, and his pace quickens. He wraps his arms around me the moment he reaches me and lifts me into his arms, spinning me around. "Ugh, I've missed you, Melly."

"Missed you too." My feet touch the floor as Julien sets me down. "How was Spain?"

"Beautiful, but I missed my friends." He shrugs like going away is not a big experience. "How's my school treating you?"

"Good actually. I've made some friends and whatnot."

My father clears his throat, catching our attention. The chair scrapes against the wooden floor as he pushes it back and stands. He walks over to us, his gaze examining my face. "You didn't walk all the way here from campus, did you?"

That was the plan until Cassius found out. He offered to drop me off, but Declan stole the keys, saving me from having to explain everything. "No, my friend dropped me off."

My father hums, dismissing the conversation. His arm wraps around my shoulder, pulling me over to the dining room table. I sit across from my brother who returns to his seat. My mom's heels click as she enters the room, carrying her usual floral ceramic pan. "I'm so glad you could make it, Julien. You know there's always room at the table for you."

"I appreciate that, Viola." He doesn't say anything else, nor does he look in our father's direction. My mother is much more accepting of Julien than he is because of a broken heart and a fragile ego.

"How is your mother?" She asks, taking a seat on the other end of the table. My mother folds her hands. Her brown hair is tied up in a clean bun with no flyaways. Her green silk dress, the one my father gave her for their anniversary, wraps perfectly around her small figure. "She's doing well I hope?"

"Yeah. She's doing fine. My stepdad is keeping her happy." It's a jab at our father. I know it is.

"Step-mother," my father *corrects*.

"James," My mother scolds my father, trying to calm the situation down. There's no use though. The damage has been done as usual.

"Alex is a man." Julien snaps his attention to our father. "Just because you don't have respect for him or the community doesn't mean he isn't more of a man than you."

"Yes, well." My mother clears her throat. "I'm happy that both your mother and step-father are doing well. Let's eat."

The rest of our Thanksgiving dinner is quiet. No one talks. Not even my parents, until a pair of footsteps, draw our attention. My brother's jaw ticks as he notices the person walking in. "You have some nerve showing your face here after my sister dumped you."

I don't bother turning, not when I'm frozen in my seat. I keep my gaze on my brother, in case he decides to do anything drastic. Not that Jay wouldn't deserve it.

"Always a pleasure, Julien. Mr. Watson, thank you for inviting me." The chair beside mine screeches over the hardwood floor.

"James, I thought we agreed not to have Melody's ex-boyfriend join us," my mother speaks.

"I think the man deserves another chance."

Seriously?

My hands curl into fists and I push myself up from my seat. "He doesn't deserve a chance. Do you even know what he did to me?"

My father nods. "I do. It was an honest mistake. He sees the error of his ways—"

"I'm not giving him another chance," I say. "I'm seeing someone."

"You are?" Jay asks with a hint of anger in his voice.

"Oh, is it that basketball player?" My mother lights up.

"What basketball player?" Julien drops another question into the pile I don't feel like answering.

"No, it's someone else."

"Come on, Mel, you can't be serious. I-I came all this way for you."

"No one asked you to. I broke it off. You made a bet and I didn't want to be a part of that."

"It's over," Jay tries to remedy the situation. "I swear, I don't care about that. I just want you."

He reaches out for me, but I move back. "You do know I heard you one night in your room, right? I was hiding under the bed."

"That's just guy talk."

"You were fucking some other girl."

Jay reaches out once again. This time my brother shoots up from his seat.

"You need to leave before I kick you out."

"Julien. Jay," my mother tries to plead, "There's no need for any of this."

"No, there isn't," my father adds as if my mom needs any help. He looks to Julien and clears his throat. "You've overstayed your welcome."

"Seriously?" Julien lets out a scoff, shaking his head. "You'll kick out your own son before someone who's treating your daughter like shit? Wow." He laughs and rounds the table, stopping at my mother. He briefly hugs her, giving her a peck on the cheek. "Thank you for inviting me, Viola. I look forward to doing this again next year."

Julien makes his way to me. His hand takes mine, a soft apologetic smile on his face. My eyes swell with tears.

It's always like this... they get into an argument for something—anything—and then my brother gets kicked out.

I squeeze his hand, not wanting him to leave but I know he won't stay. "I'm going with you."

"No, you're not," my father belts. "You're staying here and having dinner with your mother and me."

Shaking my head, I look at my mom. She gives me a small nod, showing me she understands and that's all the motivation I need.

Without a word to my father or Jay, I glance up at my brother. His eyes are filled with worry. He knows better than I do that if I leave, there's only going to be more problems. But our father should know—I'd choose someone accepting.

Julien squeezes me and pulls out of the house. For a while, he doesn't speak. Not even when he helps me into his car. He closes the door, makes it to his side, hops in, and turns on the car, driving down the road.

"Where are we going?" I finally ask the moment we turn down my street.

"A friend's house. They invited me and they're way more accepting than *him*." His grip tightens around the steering wheel. "They'll love you, Melly. Just as much as they love me. I know it."

WE'RE SEEING EACH OTHER

CASSIUS

The front door opens and a familiar face peeks through. A wide grin spreads across his face as he catches me looking over from the couch in the living room.

"Hey! Long time no see." Julien steps inside, sliding off the black beanie from his head and revealing his dirty blond hair. "Deck or Cass?"

A chuckle leaves my lips. He never could tell us apart. Then again, why would he? He moved away and mostly hung around Declan.

"Cass," I inform him and stand up. There are small movements behind him.

He seems to notice too because he looks back and says something to whoever he's with. He reaches behind and pulls them forward.

My heart drops to the floor along with my jaw.

Melody?

"This is my—"

"Please don't say girlfriend," the sentence slips from my

mouth before I have the chance to fully think anything through.

She's gripping onto the sleeves of his sweater, keeping her head low. Something inside me ticks. It's like an alarm, or a bomb ready to go off. I don't like the way she's holding on to him as if he's her lifeline.

Fuck. Is this Jay, her ex? He can't be. Fuck, I hope not. Julien has always been cool with us. I'd hate for her to be the reason we're no longer friends.

"Julien!" My brother calls as he rushes over to them from the kitchen. He dabs him up and gives him a short, but tight hug.

Declan takes a step back. He slowly tilts his head towards Melody. "How do you two know each other?"

"I've known her all her life," Julien admits. "How do you know Melly?"

"She's Cass's roommate." He leans forward like he's going to tell Julien a secret but instead, he says it loud enough for all of us to hear. "And they're kind of dating."

"Dating?" Julien's gaze moves from Declan to me. There's a primal protective instinct in them. I know it all too well. It's the same one Declan gives off when people try to get too close to Ophelia. He then drags his attention to Melody, "He's the guy you're seeing?"

Melody bites her bottom lip, nodding her head. "We haven't gone on a date yet, but…"

Her hesitation does nothing to calm the jealous rage rattling inside me.

"We're seeing each other," I say, moving off of the couch. I make my way to them by the door, sliding beside Declan. "Is that a problem?"

Julien raises an eyebrow. I'm ready to receive a snarl or for him to spit in my face, but instead he throws his head back and laughs. "Thank god it's not Declan. No offense."

"Did Melody come back from her parents yet?" My sister calls out as one of the doors in the house slams shut. I turn on my heels catching Cece stopping midway. Her smile drops the moment she sees Julien and Melody.

"Hey, don't think we've met before," Julien mentions a little too flirtatious for my liking. Though he hasn't seen Cece since she transitioned. "I'm Julien. Guess you know my sister already."

"That's Ceas—" Cece shoves into Declan, stopping him from talking.

"I'm Cece."

"Cece..." He smirks, looking between Declan and me. "Isn't that what we used to call little Caesar? Where is that little shit anyway?"

"He's not here anymore." Cece shrugs. I'm not sure why she's not telling him. She's usually much more forward in letting everyone in our past know. However, it's her choice. She doesn't have to say anything if she doesn't want to.

Julien's face pales, dread filling his eyes.

"Not like that." Cece grabs his arm and drags him away. "I'll fill you in."

Declan follows and I'm left with Melody. She fiddles with her fingers, not taking a second glance at me. "I knew Julien had a half-sister. Didn't think it was you."

She lets out what sounds like a half scoff and a half laugh. "We don't see each other much, but we talk about everything."

"Except for me." I slide my hands into my pockets, rocking on my heels. Insecurities eat away at my stomach, a sour taste erupting in the back of my throat.

"I just didn't want to say anything until after. In case it didn't go well and you changed your mind."

My eyebrows furrow. "Why would I?"

She still has yet to look at me. Those beautiful moonlight eyes are glued to her pointer fingers tapping away at each other. My hand slides out of my pocket and cups her cheek. Running my thumb against her jawline, I tilt her chin upward.

"Melody," I say softly, "look at me."

Her gaze drags over my lips and the rest of my face until her moonlight eyes meet mine. Fear lingers deep within them. My other arm finds its way around her waist, closing the space between us. "Why would I change my mind?"

"Because your ex was basically this beautiful model and I'm just me."

"You've got to stop talking about yourself like that," I warn her, not able to stand the way she can dismiss herself so easily.

There's so much more to her than just what lies on the surface. She might not see it, but I do. I might have told her, but it seems as though it still hasn't clicked. Melody is so much more than she thinks.

I want her to love herself just the way she is.

"Like what? It's true." Her voice drops, sadness seeping through. "I am just me."

"No, Moonlight," I whisper against her lips. Her breath hitches, gaze falling to my mouth. Good, I want her to pay close attention. "You are so much more. I know you can't see it and it fucking kills me that you don't. It'll take a while."

My forehead presses to hers and I gently rub our noses together. Her gaze drifts back up to mine, full of want... need. I'm trying to be the man she deserves but with the way she's looking at me and those pouty red lips, it's hard not to be tempted by her. Still, I continue my little speech. "When you finally see you are so much more than you think, you won't need me around just to tell you how beautiful you are. Inside and out."

"Are you ever going to kiss me, Cassius?" she whispers.

I ignore the feel of our friends and family staring in our direction from behind me. Nosy bastards. All of them.

With our lips a hair's breadth away, I rub my nose against hers again. "It's getting really hard not to."

I brush my lips across hers, barely touching. She smiles into my mouth.

"That's all you get," I tell her.

"Are you shy?" she asks.

"No." My fingers twitch against her lower back, aching to dive lower. "If I start kissing you, we'd need privacy for what would happen next. There's no way it would stop at kissing. Not when I've imagined your body under mine countless times after our first time together."

"I think my underwear is officially soaked."

"What?" I bark, hoping I heard right. That my dick isn't just imagining things. "What did you just say?"

Her cheeks redden and she tries to look away, but I keep a firm grip on her chin. "Repeat that for me."

"I think my underwear is soaked now..." she speaks softly. Her moonlight eyes shine with lust and fuck me... I'm aching in my jeans now. "You have this sexy-time voice and it's making me all hot and bothered."

I squeeze my eyes shut. "And now I'm here with a hard-on."

"Really?" A wicked smile grows on her lips as she giggles. "You're kidding right?" She examines my face. "If I keep talking will you—"

I press my lips to hers, hard. She lets out a little moan. Her mouth opens, inviting my bottom lip between hers. My teeth nibble at her flesh. I tug just a bit and lap my tongue over the small pain I may have inflicted on her.

"Keep it up and I might just have to take you right here with your brother in the other room hearing you scream my name." I pull away first. The taste of her lips lingers on mine. A part of me no longer cares if they know she made me rock hard or even if they hear us.

Because I'm far too eager to hear the sweet little sounds Melody lets out when she's being pleased.

"Stop trying to fuck my sister and let's have dinner," Julien calls from the living room. A chuckle leaves my lips just as a small giggle leaves Melody's.

"I'd much rather skip to dessert," I whisper. I take a step back, looking down at the sweet blush spreading across Melody's cheeks.

"I should... cool down."

"There's a pool in the garage that'll get you nice and cool or toasty, but you'll probably get wet too."

"I don't think that matters," she mumbles trying to cover it off with a cough. Melody shakes her head and tugs on my hand—leading me over toward the family.

Ophelia is sitting on the armrest, Deck beside her on the couch with his arm around her waist. Julien and Cece are seated beside him—every eye on us.

"So then... are you two official?" Cece grins from ear to ear.

I look at Melody, her moonlight eyes meeting with mine. Everything in me wants to say yes, we are. But I can see the hesitation in her gaze much like she could probably sense it in my own. She shifts her attention first, smiling at our family.

"How about we get past the first date before we really decide on anything?" Melody tells them.

"I like that idea," I say as a smile comes to my lips. My arm wraps around her waist, tugging her right where she belongs—close to me.

I just hope I can one day be enough for her.

26

I'VE SEEN BIGGER

MELODY

Cassius mentioned he had a pool in the garage the other week, a heated pool. And since I need some inspiration for Sergio and Aria's pool scene, I decided to utilize it.

I push the door open to the garage, for the first time. My gaze falls almost immediately on Cassius. Water drips from his dark hair and the tattoos inked on his skin. There is no denying Cassius is a handsome man, but there's so much more to him than just that.

Cassius is sunlight. He breathes in darkness, exhaling the light wherever he goes. Even with his back turned toward me, warmth fills every part of my body just by the mere sight.

We hadn't seen much of each other since Thanksgiving. He'd been busy with work and catching up with late assignments—which was fine. I'd been busy with Aria's story.

But now we're here.

Alone and together.

I creep in silently, peeling my eyes from the gorgeous man.

However, it does nothing to ease the heat rising to my face or the beating of my chest.

Cassius turns slowly in the water, steam rising. But I can see him clearly as the water glistens over his skin, shimmering against the fluorescent lights.

"I see you found the pool," he says. His sunlight eyes burn, lighting my body on fire as they trail down taking in the black bikini I'd gotten just before school started. My hand comes to my arm rubbing over my skin for comfort.

His Adam's apple bobs as his gaze moves back up. "Hope it's not too big for your liking."

I hum, taking a step toward him. "I've seen bigger."

A smirk grows at the corner of his lips. Eyes sparkling with humor. "Are you going to come in?"

Instead of answering him, I make my way closer. Our eyes lock, and suddenly it's harder to breathe, but I keep going anyway. He follows my every move, taking his time to inch closer to the edge of the pool, reaching it at the same time I do.

"It's not too deep is it?" I ask.

"Promise even if it is, I got you."

I lower myself down and sit at the edge of the pool. "Most garages aren't this warm."

"There's a lot of things about this garage and house that aren't like most," he tells me. I tilt my head, urging him to continue and he does. "Well, the in-ground pool for one. It's only here because Mr. Monroe, our landlord, installed it for his daughter. She loved the water so he got this pool."

"He must really love her."

"He does. Her and the rest of his family. This place was actually for his daughter."

"So why do you live here?"

"Neither of his kids wanted the house. And since Mr. Monroe knew I was looking for something off campus, he gave me the keys. It also helped I've known him for years." He shrugs.

Cassius doesn't talk much about himself or those around him, I've noticed, but when he does… I listen. I want to know about him, his life, the people he holds close to his heart. I just want to keep learning about him.

"I used to work in Mr. Monroe's tattoo parlor, just cleaning things up until I was old enough to practice. He even handed over his tattoo shop and told me to rename it—make it my own. They're… they're the parents I never had growing up."

I lower myself down and sit. Cassius moves closer, in between my legs. His arm wraps around my waist, eyes staring up at me, so full of kindness and patience. My fingers brush through his damp hair. My feet in the water. It's not too cold, not on my toes, at least.

"Were you looking for me?" he asks.

I shake my head. "No. I didn't think you would be here actually."

"Sometimes, I use it at night." He shrugs his shoulders. "Mostly when I need to think. Besides, I can look at the stars sometimes."

I blink twice. My gaze drifts over to the closed garage door. "That would be a beautiful sight. The stars glistened in the water."

"The ceiling actually opens," he mentions, giving me space to move. "Behind you on the wall, there's two switches. It's the one on to your right."

I push back and stand to do exactly that. The ceiling parts, letting in the glistening stars and the light of the full moon.

I keep my on the sky as I walk back over to the pool. "My family doesn't have this... A pool with a view I mean." I sit back down, sliding slowly into the pool.

"My family never had a pool." He looks up, taking in the sky. "We barely could afford anything. This place was a steal, to be honest."

Lowering myself back down, I sit as he slowly moves toward me again. "So, if you're not here for me, what are you here for?"

"Inspiration."

"Aria's story?" He raises an eyebrow with a smile.

I hum, lowering my gaze to my thighs. My eyebrows draw together. I don't know how to explain it, but I try anyway. "There's this scene where Aria walks in on Sergio in the pool and he touches her, but..."

"How does he touch her?"

"Huh?"

Cassius's hands splay over my thighs, thumb caressing my skin. Warmth spreads through my body. My gaze drifts upward, meeting his. A silent plea lingers in them and my legs part. His grip tightens pulling me closer to the edge while he inches further between my legs.

"Well, she wants to be normal," I say, letting him wrap his arms around my waist. My hands come to his shoulder as he helps me down into the pool. His sunlight eyes keep mine hostage. It's a certain sense of intimacy I've never known. Looking into someone's eyes while speaking—I could never do such a thing. But with Cassius, I want to—I want to reveal all the secrets I've hidden in the pages of my stories. "She wants to feel normal for once. Like who she is... what she's been through no longer exists."

"Is that what you want too, Moonlight?" His voice is low,

breath mingles with mine. "To feel like nothing else in the world exists?"

I nod, my gaze still locked on his.

"I need words, Moonlight. Tell me what you want."

"I want to feel normal again. Brave. Loved. Cherished. Like that night we had."

His head dips lips trace along my neck and over my jawline until they reach my lips, setting my entire body on fire. He pulls me into him. Our bodies fit perfectly, but all I can really focus on is his lips against mine. The way my mouth opens freely, giving him and his tongue access, and after a moment of hesitation, mine follows his.

I swallow the groan leaving his mouth. His hands move over my body; caressing, gripping, marking me. He pulls from our kiss, eyes dark and full of lust. "You remember your promise?"

His forehead presses to mine, hands grabbing mine and wrapping them around his neck.

"Anytime you want to stop." He presses his lips to mine. His hands lower, sliding around my waist. "Tell me, and I will."

27

CONFIDENT, PLEASED, AND THOROUGHLY SATISFIED

CASSIUS

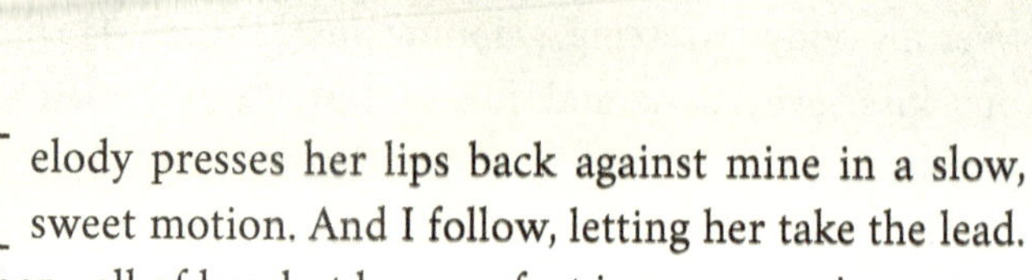

Melody presses her lips back against mine in a slow, sweet motion. And I follow, letting her take the lead. I want her—all of her, but her comfort is way more important to me than my desires.

Much like our one night together, our kiss picks up. She's eager. No longer shy or nervous.

My fingers move between us, lowering over her stomach and down to her waist. Those fucking strings hanging the sides, keeping her bottoms together—gone within seconds. My hand grips her thigh, wrapping her leg around me. I push into her, feeling the heat of her pussy through my swim shorts.

Fuck I need her.

I need her like I need the oxygen in my lungs to breathe. Like I need water to survive.

"You feel that, Moonlight?" I tell her pushing into her again. "You feel how hard you make me?"

The most seductive sound falls from her lips and I press my mouth to hers, tasting and savoring all of those sweet and sexy as fuck sounds she's giving.

I pull from our kiss, eyes on hers as I trail my two fingers over her skin, sliding further down. Her eyes close as my thumb rubs against her sensitive bud, but I don't stop letting my fingers explore, dipping into her sweet pussy.

"Fuck, you feel incredible around my fingers, Moonlight."

Her hips rock and I follow that rhythm, playing with her body, stroking each cord I can find that makes my beautiful Melody sing. And sing she does.

"Cassius," she manages to let out.

"Yes, Moonlight?"

"I want you inside me."

"Is that really what you want, Moonlight? Me, deep inside you, fucking that sweet pussy of yours until you cum all over my cock?"

She throws her head back and I sink my fingers deeper, faster, harder. My mouth laches onto her neck, sucking on that one spot at the base of her neck. She whimpers, her body tensing. "Let it go, baby, cum for me, Moonlight."

She topples over the edge, eyes closing. Her sweet voice filling every inch of the garage. My pace slows, easing her down from her high. Pink coats her cheeks, lips parted as she tries to catch her breath.

I pepper kisses along her jaw, my dick hard as a rock, aching with need. My grip on her waist loosens, and I'm hoping I didn't leave a bruise on her.

Yet the thought of my mark on her skin has my dick pulsing even more.

"How was that for inspiration?" I whisper against her neck.

She tilts her head. Moonlight eyes meet mine. Her mouth curls into a smile, and fuck—I swear I would give anything to see her like this all the time.

Confident, pleased, and thoroughly satisfied.

"I think I'm going to need some more," she says, a giggle following after.

I can't help but chuckle.

She's infected me, inked my soul with everything she does, everything she says, every time she looks at me.

I'm hers. Completely and utterly hers.

I grab her hand, lifting it to my mouth. My lips brush over her knuckles. "Maybe after our first date."

"We've already had sex."

I shake my head. "*That* was a one-time thing, Moonlight. The next time it's going to be more. Because this time, you're mine and I'm not letting you go."

"You're not saying we can't have sex."

A groan leaves my lips. *She's so...fuck.* I can't even put it into words. I want to say fuck it, give her what she wants, and fuck her right here inside this pool, but I want to give her more than that. "Let me be a gentleman and take you on a date first."

Melody pouts, looking away before glancing up at me from under her eyelashes. "Can we... at least shower together?"

I smile, tugging on her bottom lip. "You can shower with me whenever you want, Moonlight. My doors are always open."

For her, at least.

"And our date?"

"I cleared my whole schedule," I tell her, a smile forms on

my lips as I take her other hand in mine. "This weekend, I'm all yours."

MEANT TO BE MINE

MELODY

I shouldn't be nervous about a date with Cassius. He's possibly the nicest guy I've ever met. Yet, I can't help the way my nerves rattle under my skin. It's not like we haven't been out before. Though, this time, I'm not sure where we're going or if we're still going.

Cassius said an hour, but he's been in his room for longer.

My doors are always open.

Deciding to test his theory, I turn the knob and push the door open.

His room is covered in darkness for the most part. Light shines through the windows making it easier for me to look around. The carpet is cleared, unlike mine covered in clothes, and the blue covering his walls are bare. There's no personality in this room. It's almost as if it isn't even his. Like this isn't his place, just somewhere he rests for a few hours.

And I guess that's true.

Maybe one day that'll change.

Cass lays on his bed. His arm rests over his face as his

chest rises and falls. I walk into the room and climb onto the bed. Sitting beside him, I brush my fingers over his arm. Cassius shoots up, his hand takes hold of my wrists. He opens his eyes and looks at me.

"Shit, Melody." He huffs out, loosening his grip. "I'm sorry."

He brings my wrists to his lips, placing a soft gentle kiss on both.

"You fell asleep," I tell him. "Long day?"

He hums, pulling me down gently with him. I lay beside him, resting my head on his chest. His fingers comb through my hair, loosening the curls I just finished getting done. But I don't care. Not with the way he holds me close like he never wants to let go or the way his heart beats against my ear drums.

And with his arm holding me tight, I don't think I even want him to let go.

He makes me feel all kinds of things. Feelings I never thought were possible. And more than anything, he makes me feel seen, cared for and loved.

"What time is it now?" he asks.

"Just a little after six," I say.

"Fuck, I didn't mean to nap for so long." He groans, pressing a small kiss to the top of my head. "We should get going before they close."

"Where are we going exactly?" I swing my leg over, climbing on top of him.

"Somewhere you'll love." His hands make their way to my hips. He slides them over my curves, his eyes taking in every inch of me. "But we won't get there this way."

Cassius smiles, thrusting his hips into me. I fall forward. My hands spread on his chest, catching myself. "And don't say you'd rather be here, under me, or in your room writing. We're going out."

I chuckle as he helps me off him. I plant my feet on the ground as he sits up. "Okay, fine. But I was supposed to take you out, remember?"

"I do remember." His finger tugs on the belt loop of my jeans. His sunlight eyes melt my insides. "The thing is, I really want to make this date special."

"For a little then," I tell him. "It's supposed to rain."

He slides his hand into mine, giving it a gentle squeeze. "Trust me, you'll want more than just a little time."

Cassius stands, patting his pants and making sure he has everything. Once he's convinced he does, his arm around my waist, pulling me close.

Ever since the night in the pool, he's kept me as close as he can whenever we cross paths.

I'm not complaining. Not when those sunlight eyes stare at me, igniting my body on fire. And the sweetness that comes out of his mouth—I can't help but want more.

"If you want to leave after you see the place, I'll make it up to you any way you want."

I glance over at him. Lust fills those sunlight eyes making my insides melt. I lose my voice and nod in response.

It's like he was crafted with one thought in mind...

He was meant to be mine.

MY EYES ARE STILL SHUT the moment the car stops moving. The engine cuts off and the soft touch of Cass's hand has me turning my head in his direction. "Keep them closed, Moonlight. I'm gonna grab you."

His hand moves from mine. The door opens, letting the cold air of early December slip inside before he shuts it. He doesn't take long to open my side. His fingers grip my wrist, helping me out of the car. "Can I open them now?"

"No." He chuckles, shutting the door behind me. He pulls me with him, leading me to the place he said I'd love. How true is that? I'm not sure. But I can hear small chatters in the distance, car engines starting and stopping. It must be a place lots of people go to. Maybe a shopping mall? The store?

"Okay," he finally says. "You can open them."

My eyes flutter open on command.

The largest bookstore in our area stands three floors tall before me. The building is covered in white paint and the blue letters read: Books 'n Nooks.

It's a place I've always wanted to go to but never had the time. A place my parents never took me. A place I only ever dreamed of visiting.

Three floors—full of everything I could ever want.

Slowly, I turn my head toward Cassius, he's staring back at me. A giddy smile on his face.

"How did you know I'd want to come here?"

"What do you mean, how'd I know?" He leans over, pressing his soft lips to my cheek. "You're a writer. Of course, you'd love coming to a bookstore. If not for the books, for the writer goodies they probably have around."

My chest bubbles with warmth, ready to explode. My arms wrap around his neck, keeping him close. His arms do the same to my waist as his face nuzzles into my neck.

"I've always wanted to come here," I mumble against his skin. "But never could."

He pulls away, only enough to press our foreheads together. "It's a good thing you have me to take you to all the places you've wanted to go, huh?"

A small giggle leaves my lips. "You really know a way into a girl's heart."

"I try." He steals a kiss and then stands up straight. My hands fall from his neck. He takes one in his, weaving our fingers together. His hand practically covers mine and I can't complain.

With him by my side, I feel as though everything else doesn't exist. The only thing that matters is the way I feel when I'm with him:

Like I'm somebody important.

29

TOO PERFECT TO BE TRUE

CASSIUS

Every time Melody picks up an item–carries it around, and then places it down–I grab whatever it is and hold it for her. The hardcover edition of Grimm's Fairy Tales she places back in its spot? I take it from the shelf and hold it with the rest of the pile I have in my hand.

She turns on her heels, placing her fists on her waist. A pout comes to her lips as her gaze drifts to the ten books in my hands.

"Why do you keep grabbing them?" she asks like it's a terrible burden to hold what she seems to want until her eyes fall on the price.

I raised an eyebrow at her. "Are you going to buy them?"

Melody glances back at the books in my hand, eying each one again like she's contemplating on if she really wants them or not. She sighs, her shoulders dropping. "No."

"Ok," I say, "then I will."

"Do you even read?" She means if I even read these types

of books. The eight romances she picked out, the fairytale book, and the one random fantasy cover which she squealed about because it was on the retelling table.

"Who said they're for me?" I flash her a smile. Her face drops, her eyes searching mine.

"Cassius," she says in a warning tone.

"Moonlight." The smile on my face grows into a grin. "If you feel so bad about it, I'll let you pick from this pile before we get the register. For now, just don't pay any mind to me."

Melody keeps her gaze on mine, but I'm not backing down. Not one bit. If she wants these books, she's going to get them.

We continue through the bookshop, hitting the third floor. I grab a basket at the top of the escalator and place the books in carefully. Melody runs from me, turning into the area with pens and notebooks. Luckily there's space on the sides for anything else she wants. Worse case, I'll grab another basket.

I follow after her, toward the area of pens and notebooks. She stops in front of a table. Her fingers brush over a plain spiral notebook. There is a longing in the way she takes her time, trailing down the spine.

"It's four for a dollar," I tell her as I read the sign beside it. "Could save it for your next book ideas."

I like the way her lips curl into a smile at that statement. She bites her bottom lip, trying to keep it at bay, but there's no use. Melody picks up four and turns to me.

"I'm paying for these."

"You act as if this is too much," I reach over, brushing a single strand of hair behind her ear.

She sighs. "Jay used to say—"

My hand slides to the back of her neck, pulling her to me. I lean down, foreheads touching. My gaze bounces between her moonlight eyes. She needs to realize this now before we keep going.

"I don't care what he used to say or do, Moonlight." My lips brush gently against hers. "He's not your man."

Neither are you.

I try to ignore the sting the thought sends to my heart. "If you're worried about money, I got it covered."

"No—yes, but," she sighs, struggling.

"Melody," I press my lips to hers. "I want to spoil you. I want to see that pretty smile on your face every second of the day. I want you to be happy and I want to be the one who always makes you feel that way."

"Okay," Melody says, placing her hand on my arm. She holds it as she takes a step back.

She's not smiling. I pray she's just confused. Unsure because her dick of an ex never treated her the way I am. I hope that's all this is and not her wanting to steer clear of me.

My insecurities creep up my stomach, but the moment her hand slides into mine, they crawl back down. I breathe in, relieved, and bring her hand to my lips, brushing it over her knuckles.

Patters can be heard from the ceiling like someone is dropping rice into a bucket carefully and then, it falls. My gaze drifts toward the nearest window. Sheets of rain fall from the sky.

"Told you."

That she did, but a little rain doesn't hurt. Though, I might have to ask the cashier for an extra bag to keep her stuff from getting ruined. Still… "We should probably get going before it gets worse."

"RACE YOU," Melody says the minute we step out of the store. She sprints toward the car and I rush after her. The pouring rain drenches me the minute my feet hit the street. She's running, squealing with delight as she spins on her heels. Once. Twice. And then walks with a pep in her step. I slow down and match her pace. I wrap my arm around her shoulder, leading her to the car with one hand while the other hangs onto the bag of books.

By the time we reach the car, my entire body is soaked. My shirt sticks to my skin and my hair is dripping. I open the car door for her, but instead of getting in, she laughs.

Her head is tilted to the sky, hands open wide, inviting the pouring rain to wet her even more.

"Moonlight, you're going to get sick."

"Have you ever danced in the rain before?" she asks as if she didn't even hear what I said. She lowers her head, looking at me. The smile on her face is infectious.

I shake my head, not able to say I ever did. Cara hated the rain. It always made her hair frizz up. She would always wait until the rain died down to leave. I place the books into the car and turn to her, holding my hand out.

"Really?" She glances at my hand and then up at me. Her eyes are wide, full of wonder.

I nod my head, letting her slide her hand into mine. I give her a twirl as my arm wraps around her waist. She steps back, and I follow her lead, dancing in the middle of a practically empty parking lot by my car, in the rain.

But she's smiling and I'll dance every fucking time in the rain if I can always see her this happy—this tree.

Both of my arms wrap around her waist as I spin us both. She leans back, letting her head drop as she laughs.

I pull her back up, and her hands land on my shoulder. Those beautiful moonlight eyes stare back at me. "I like you a lot, Melody."

She smiles up at me, almost as if she knows I'm not done. Not even close.

"So I was wondering if you'll give me a chance to make you the happiest person in the world. Say you'll be mine."

She lifts herself up on her toes, pressing her lips softly to mine. It's the sweetest kiss I've ever gotten. I melt into her, caging her in my grasp.

I pull apart first, resting my forehead on hers.

"You're too perfect to be true," she whispers.

"I'm far from it, Moonlight, but I'm hoping that means the answer's a yes. "Please tell me it's a yes."

She laughs. "How can I say no when you danced with me and kissed me in the rain?"

"I also walked around each floor carrying all the books you wanted."

"You also bought them." She shakes her head. Her gaze meets with mine again. "I write books imagining what it would be like if a guy like you existed and now here you are."

"And I don't plan on going anywhere, Moonlight." I give her one last kiss before I lower my arms from her waist. "Now get in the car before we get sick."

Melody pouts, but only for a brief moment before she smiles and does as I say.

Closing the door, I walk over to my side, getting drenched

and dripping. None of that matters though. Not when I have my moonlight beside me.

I'm the luckiest guy to be able to call her mine.

30

BE BRAVE, BE BOLD

MELODY

A knock at my door has me looking up from my textbook. Notes scatter my desk, pinned with sticky notes highlighting important information to focus on. It's been like this for a week. Studying with no time for anything else.

My head pounds, mimicking the sound of the knocks. But I need to get all of this done. However, the impatient person on the other side of the door pushes it open before I can get there.

Cece appears from behind. A Cheshire grin on her face, until she looks at the mess beside me. "Girl. You need a break."

A break sounded nice, for someone who's been in class all semester. Even though I'd only missed a week I've yet to catch up on all the assignments and tests.

Cece walks over, and her fingers grab one of my essays for literature. "Aren't you into reading and writing?"

"With classes like these, I have to analyze text so there's more to it. I can't just enjoy the experience of reading."

She hums, placing the paper back down. "And how much do you have to finish?"

My gaze scans the two textbooks, four notebooks, and various papers. "About 3. The others I finished."

She shakes her head. "Give me an hour. Just one hour and you can hide back in your hole. Deal?"

I sigh, knowing there isn't a way to get out of it even if I want to. A break sounded like a good idea with my head spinning. "Sure. Where are we going?"

"Have you eaten yet?" My grumbling stomach answers for me, making Cece laugh. "We can go to Inked Hearts. Declan said he saved a box of pizza and wings for me. We can share."

My eyebrows draw together. It feels like a setup. She's trying to get me to the tattoo shop. But why? "Did Cassius put you up to this?"

"Maybe." She winks. "But you didn't hear it from me."

I glance at the scattered papers and textbooks at my desk begging me to finish so it can be done—over with. However, my heart tugs me in Cece's direction. Cassius wants to see me.

And that sounds way more important and fun.

Maybe it'll help me concentrate more or maybe it'll be too much of a distraction.

I shake the thoughts from my head. These textbooks aren't going anywhere. It's time for me to be bold, be brave, and be ballsy.

And maybe a little irresponsible for a change.

"Ok fine," I say. Without any hesitation, Cece takes my hand and drags me out.

When we arrive at the tattoo shop, Declan is standing outside with his pink cap on as usual. His eyes skate over my attire; leggings, an oversized university, and my fuzzy slippers Cece refused to let me change out of.

"I guess it'll be easy for Cass to strip you out of those." He shrugs.

My face burns, body freezing. *Does he know? Do they know that we...* My face must say it all because he chuckles and shakes his head. "I'm not even going to ask. I'm just going to assume you got what you needed."

That's one way to put it.

Declan opens the door for me. "Go on in. He's waiting for you at his station."

My feet move forward and I take in the framed drawings on the wall. Each one is unique in its own way. I wonder which ones belong to Cass, but I don't linger on the thought.

The smell of grease and pepperoni fills my senses as soft music plays from the speakers. The same one when I stepped into Inked Hearts six months ago; Dirty Little Secret by The All American Rejects.

"The first day I met you, you came in for a tattoo." Cassius's voice grabs my attention from the hall.

My gaze finds him, leaning against the doorframe of his station. His lips curl into a bright smile and my heart begins to race.

"And the second time we crossed paths, I couldn't resist making you mine, even if it meant I never got to see you again."

I'm drawn in, following his voice that hypnotizes me like a siren's call. His hand finds mine, lacing our fingers together as he leads me into his station. "You never did explain why you were alone at the bar after."

"My... the thoughts of my characters being bold convinced me to go out for the night. I wanted to make the time here memorable."

Cassius turns toward me, our gazes meeting. "Was it?"

He knows it was, or at least I feel as though he should. But there's a speck of sadness in his eyes, one that makes me think he might not be so sure. It tugs at my heartstrings, forcing me to answer with a simple nod.

A smile grows on his lips as he helps me sit on the tattoo bed. "Good, because it was for me too. The thing is," he stands in front of me, fingers tugging at the hem of my sweater. "I noticed you never got that tattoo."

His sunlight eyes quietly ask me to take it off and I do. Captivated, my gaze never leaves his as I let it fall to the floor. Cassius kicks his stool over and sits down.

"Moonlight," he whispers, nearly begging. "You have to stop looking at me like that right now."

"Like what?"

"Like you want a repeat of that night here."

I mean, I wouldn't say no.

He raises an eyebrow like he can read my mind. He scoffs playfully and shakes his head. "I wanted you to come here so I can show you everything I've been working on since then."

"For me?" I ask.

"Yes, for you." Cassius takes my hand in his. "If you still want a tattoo."

I blink twice, suddenly realizing he doesn't know. "I can't get one."

"No?" he asks. Shaking my head, I lower my gaze to our hands.

"I still want to show you." He grabs the sketchbook beside me and places it on my lap, opening up to a typewriter shaded in with letters flying out. They spell out a word... or maybe words.

Be brave, be bold, be ballsy.

My eyes widen as my attention drifts to his face. "How did you know…"

"Cece told me about your little mantra. Thought it'd look nice going around this scar." He rubs his thumb gently over the *S*-shaped scar on my left arm. "The typewriter would sit at the base of it, so it looks like it's going up your hand."

He flips the page, showing me an open book and quill beside it. Behind is a stack of books, one being Aria, Mafia Princess.

"That's not the name of the book," I tell him. "It doesn't have one yet."

"Well, when you figure it out let me know and I'll change it."

My finger traces the outline of the drawing. There's shading and detail. He clearly put a lot of thought and effort into these. It's a shame I can't have them on my skin.

"Have you ever considered a temporary tattoo?"

"You mean like the ones you find in a jar for a quarter?"

"Something like that." Cassius smiles and I can't seem to keep myself from doing the same. "Lay back and hold your arms out."

I raise an eyebrow curiously but do as he says anyway. He takes his sketches, walks away, and then returns. I eye him as he gently turns my wrist and places a clear piece of paper with a stenciled drawing on it. He holds it in place for a few moments before slowly peeling it off. And then he does the same adding a thinner piece below.

"All set."

I lift my arm, taking in the black splatters around a pink anatomical heart. *His logo* for this space he made his home was now marked on my skin. And below it is my mantra; *Be brave, be bold, be ballsy.*

"It might be temporary, and only last about a week or so," he says, "but that doesn't mean you are."

My gaze finds those sunlight eyes. Its fire burns every negative thought trying to make its way through.

"And now we can kind of match."

"Match?" I ask

Cassius holds out his arm. Right where the dragon opens his mouth, a tongue sticks out unlike before. However, as I look closer, it's not a tongue. It's my mantra.

"Figured I need to do the same too." Cassius tugs on my hand, helping me sit up. He moves between my legs and places his hands on my thighs. "I know we already live together, but I was thinking, maybe we can share a room instead."

"You want me to move into your space?"

"Or I move into yours if you want. If you aren't comfortable just yet we don't have to."

"No! I want to."

"Yeah?" His smile blossoms into a full-blown grin.

"With you, I want to take every chance." I wrap my arms around his neck and press my lips to his. "Is that okay?"

"Of course, it's more than okay, Moonlight."

I can't help the smile growing on my lips. The only thing left for us to do was to tell my parents. My skin crawls at the idea, but Cass's grip on my waist pulls me from that fear. "Will you come to meet my parents next weekend?"

He blinks twice, searching my eyes almost like he's worried. "If that's what you want, yeah. I'll meet them."

"Okay," I tell him. "We can be brave together."

Because meeting my father could break us before we even really begin.

And I really hope it doesn't.

31

YOUR PARENT'S HOUSE

CASSIUS

"We're almost there," Melody says as she tightens her grip on my hand.

Either she can sense the nerves crawling up my skin as I grip the steering wheel or she's nervous herself. Not that she has anything to worry about. She's just seeing her parents. I'm the one meeting them. I don't know anything about the two, just that her mom had been dying to meet me and her father isn't the easiest to get along with.

"You said Julien is going to be there?" I ask, hoping I'll have at least someone to be around if Melody has to leave my side for some reason.

"I told him you were going so he said he didn't want to miss out on the show."

It'll definitely be entertaining for someone and tortuous for others—mainly me. "So, is there anything I should know?"

She tilts her head, tapping her finger against her chin. "My mother is a music teacher and my father works at the school," she says before directing me over the bridge.

The *rich people* area is what my siblings and I call it. Condos upon condos, all identical to the next. But why would we be around here? "I thought you said you didn't know anyone in town."

"I never said that."

Maybe not, but she let Cece mention something along those lines. I shouldn't be mad, given the fact that we got so close in such a short time, but she could have at least mentioned it at some point even if I am usually busy. Then again, I also could have brought it up myself.

"I really didn't want to live with my parents."

"So your parents live out here?"

She nods. "I'm sorry. I should have told you."

"It's fine, Melody. But you're going to have to fill me in on what we're getting into. Is this a rich people's party or a small family dinner?"

I glance over, catching her with her head still tilted. She's thinking, maybe even unsure since she's taking so long. I pull my attention back to the road ahead.

"Knowing my parents it's a party. But I'm really hoping for something small like how Thanksgiving was."

Both are nerve-wracking no matter what. I might be good at talking to strangers at work but in a public setting? Not one bit. Especially when it came to meeting parents.

She leads me down another road, one I remember vaguely from when Cara and I used to date.

"It's the house at the top of the hill," she tells me.

Suddenly a different set of nerves spike through me. There's only one person I know who lives up there. A certain somebody who hates the living hell out of me.

"Is this your parent's house or someone else's?" I ask, searching for more clarity.

"My parents." I can feel her gaze on me, but I don't bother looking in her direction. *Melody... What was her last name anyway?* It dawns on me that I don't know her full name. We never signed an agreement for her to live with me. I also never asked her for money to rent out the room. I should have found out when she first came into my life or at least looked more thoroughly at the paperwork she gave Cece when she came in for a tattoo, but I hadn't.

"So, what am I supposed to call them?" I ask, hoping that nagging thought in the back of my brain is wrong. "Mr. And Mrs. Melody?"

"Watson."

The name nearly makes me choke. Anger slowly vibrates through me. *It's just a coincidence. She can't actually be related to him. Maybe she's a niece or something. Yeah, maybe her parents moved in.*

"What exactly does your dad do at the school, Melody?"

"He's the—" She stops herself and I glance in her direction. Her eyes are wide like she just remembered something important. "We should turn around."

"That's not an answer, Moonlight." My grip on the wheel tightens. "What does he do?"

"He's the chancellor." Her voice is soft and shaky.

My hand slams against the steering wheel. She flinches from the corner of my eyes. "I'm sorry," I breathe out.

Fuck. It's not her fault. She never knew. I never told her about my issues with the chancellor—her father. Fuck did he really have to be? When I first saw them, I thought for sure he was just showing a new student around, but he was her dad?

"I'm not..." I slide my hand from hers, running it through my hair. But it does nothing to soothe the anger coursing through me. "Seriously? He's your dad?"

Taking a glance at her, I watch as she nods her head.

"Fuck."

Being mad isn't going to change the fact that she's related to that asshole.

"I'm not mad at you, Moonlight." I sigh, letting my shoulders drop from their tense state. "Shit, if you told me sooner we wouldn't even be here."

Granted, I still have the chance to turn the car around. "Did my siblings know?"

I sneak another glance her way as she bites her lip.

Fuck.

They knew.

Of course, they knew.

"Your brothers have become friends with my daughter."

They knew and didn't even tell me. Cece and Declan let me fall for the daughter of the asshole ruining my fucking life.

"I'd hate for your establishment to be demolished due to unfortunate circumstances."

And once he knows I'm dating her, he'll make good on his promise. Everything I worked hard for is one foot away from being ripped out of my hands.

Does she know? Is this all part of some big fucking plan?

My gaze drifts over to hers. Water clouds those beautiful moonlight eyes, and as much as I want to turn this car around. I can't break her heart like that.

"Please, don't hate me."

I gently take her hand and place a small kiss on it. "I don't hate you, Moonlight. I don't like that you didn't tell me until now, but I understand we've both been preoccupied, and I never told you about my issues with him. So it's fine."

"Are we going home then?" she asks, looking up at me from under her eyelashes.

"No," I tell her, "but to be clear, I'm doing this for you, Moonlight. No one else. And if he says one word about my siblings, I won't hold back."

"I understand."

"You ready for this?" Melody asks the moment we reach the door.

I shake my head because it's the truth. I'm not, but who's ever really ready to do anything? No one. "Don't think I'll ever be."

Glancing over, I catch her frown. One of the worst sights I could ever see. I tug her gently into my side, wrap my arm around her, and press a kiss to her head. "That doesn't mean I won't do it. If meeting your family means a lot to you, I'll do it every single day."

Even though I can't stand her father.

Even if I'll lose everything I worked for.

We head inside, the door is surprisingly unlocked. She leads me down a long corridor. Da Vinci, Van Gogh, Picasso, and more bring life to the dull white painted walls. *I wonder if he's secretly into art,* which would explain his previous statement about an art gallery.

The sound of piano keys grows louder as she stops in front of a doorframe. I turn, peeking inside. There, a woman dressed in a velvet maroon dress sits in front of a grand piano. Her fingers work their way across every key needed to form a striking melody.

My own beautiful Melody tugs on my hand, bringing me

closer. The more I listen, the more I recognize a song I grew up listening to. A song I once tried to play.

Melody sits down beside the pianist, resting her head on the woman's shoulder, but keeps our fingers interlocked. I stand facing Melody's side, letting the calming music seep through my body.

The woman continues to play and our presence doesn't seem to bother her. She nears the end of the song. Her fingers slow down with each note until it stops at a low, vibrating, key.

"You always play my song on this day," Melody says.

The woman turns her head and places a small kiss on top of Melody's. "Because I played it to get you to sleep on your first birthday."

Wait... it's Melody's birthday?

The woman lifts her attention. Her eyes catch mine. She looks a lot like Melody. The dark wavy hair, the same rounded eyes, cheekbones, and pouty red lips. The only difference is her arms. "Sweetheart, I thought you were bringing your boyfriend."

Melody sits up straight and tilts her head to look at me. Her lips curve into a smile. "This is Cassius, my boyfriend. He's Declan's brother."

"Oh my, twins. I'm sorry honey," she smiles at me.

"No need to apologize, Mrs. Watson. Everyone gets us mixed up."

"Please, call me Viola." Another music name.

Footsteps slap against the marble floor and I feel sudden spikes prickling at my skin. "Melody, Viola, the party is in the dining room, not out here."

"James, come meet Melody's boyfriend." She reaches out for him. Melody squeezes my hand for support or maybe she's afraid of what's to come. Either way, I swallow hard. The moment he takes her hand and looks over, getting a glimpse at me.

His steel blue eyes narrow the minute he takes me in, challenging me. "Cassius."

"Mr. Watson." My free hand balls into a fist, chest tightening.

"So," he begins, jaw tight. "You're the man my daughter is seeing."

I nod, not afraid to admit the fact. He can threaten to take it all away, as long as I get to keep Melody. "I am."

"And how long has this been going on? Before or after we had our little talk?"

My gaze narrows. *After.* Definitely after.

"What talk?" Melody asks, turning her head towards me, but I'm dead set on keeping my attention on her father.

"He came by one day threatening to take down my tattoo shop."

"James," her mother gasps.

"I asked Mr. Valencia here to keep his family at a distance from our Melody, seeing as she's easily misguided."

"Viola," I lower my gaze to her just as she does the same. "With all due respect, your daughter is capable of making her own decisions regardless of what your husband claims."

"Wh-when did you talk to each other?" Melody asks, her voice shaky with nerves. Her grasp slips, along with her trust.

My knees give way as I bend down beside her, moving her legs until she's facing me. Tears swell in her eyes, body visibly shaking. *Shit shit... she's got it all wrong.*

"I swear it's not what you might be thinking, Moonlight. I'm not with you for any type of revenge or gain, other than your heart and trust."

Mr. Watson scoffs. "Why else would you date my daughter?"

My attention shoots right toward him—eyes narrowed, jaw clenched. This man can't be serious. His daughter is nearly ready to crawl into a hole and burst into tears, yet he's bringing each fear out into the open.

"Can I speak to you, in private?" I nearly grit out.

He nods, looking down at Melody and then at his wife. Mrs. Watson moves first, ushering Melody out with arm rubs and hopefully soothing whispers.

"Go on, tell me. What are you not man enough to say in front of my daughter?"

"I know what you want to hear." I roll my eyes and shake my head, giving him the smirk he probably expects. "I don't actually like your daughter. I'm dating her out of spite to get back at you and honestly, I just feel sorry for her."

The words leave a sour taste in my mouth. I take a step toward him, man to man. "But none of that's true. I'd never date someone out of spite and I like Melody a lot. She's a smart and beautiful person, which I'm sure she got from her mom. I feel lucky that she agreed to be with me."

"And you'd really give up your establishment for her? Because if I recall you couldn't seem to do that for your last girlfriend."

My eyebrows draw together. "How do you know about—"

"What did you say to Melody?" Julien's voice has me cutting my words short and spinning on my heels.

"What?"

"She just walked past me crying. So which one of you did it?"

I push on my feet, ready to sprint the hell out of there and get to her, but Julien steps in my way. "I asked a question, Cass. Did you hurt my sister or was it him?"

"What are *you* doing here? Shouldn't you be with your mother and her wife?" Mr. Watson asks.

"Husband. Alex is a man. I'm so sick of you disrespecting him. Viola and Melody wanted me to come by. If it wasn't for them, I wouldn't even be here."

"Your stepdad is transgender?" My gaze shifts back to Mr. Watson. "So, you've been a fucking asshole just because you can't get over the fact that your old lover found someone better who treated her right? So you decide to focus that anger on her new lover and everyone else who is a part of the community and its allies?"

Shaking my head, I give up on this conversation. It's pointless. "You know what, I don't have time for this petty bullshit. I gotta find Melody."

"Like hell you are," Julien grips my arm, holding me back.

"I didn't do shit, Jules," I tell him, yanking my arm from him. "I love her alright? Just let me go and make things right." Shoving past him, I race out of the place.

I just hope she'll listen.

32

THIS ISN'T FICTION

MELODY

"I don't actually like your daughter. I'm dating her out of spite to get back at you and honestly, I just feel sorry for her."

Cassius's words cut me like a knife, gutting me from the inside. I try not to think about it, how easily he fooled me, but the words circle in my head. Why did I ever think he was different or like the characters in my book?

My characters are flawed. They make mistakes, and there are misunderstandings. But when it comes to the woman they are with, they'll do anything to keep them. Outside obstacles are just that. They don't say horrible stuff about the other. That's not my kind of book, but it doesn't matter.

This isn't fiction, this is real life.

And girls like me, don't get happy endings. We get disappointed. We open our hearts and get trampled on. People take what they need, drain us dry, leaving us with nothing but a pit of darkness in our chests and bricks to cage our hearts in.

I swallow down the negative thoughts, but they sprout and grow even bigger than the last. The tears haven't stopped since I left my parents, since I took a ride back to campus, since I gave the driver money to help me pack my stuff—since I stood in front of Cece's dorm with all of my stuff.

I still haven't told her anything. She's just sitting quietly by my side, stroking my hair. Cece tries to soothe me with a lullaby, but it does nothing. I just want to close my eyes and be far away from here.

"Your brother is calling you... do you want to answer it?" she asks, sliding my phone next to the pillow. It illuminates, pulsing with each ring, but I don't care for it. Don't want it.

I grab it anyway, shut it down, and pull the blankets over my head.

"Melody..." her voice is desperate. "Can you just tell me what happened?"

I shake my head, burying my face into the pillow. I just want to be alone, in silence, with the darkness as my only friend.

"I just feel sorry for her."

His words wrap around my heart, suffocating my lungs. I choke out a cry, shutting my eyes tight. Crying won't get me anywhere, but it hurts. It hurts so much. I just... I thought he liked me—maybe even loved me. But I was wrong. Stupid. Of course, he doesn't like me. Of course, it was all to just get close to my dad. Of course, he just felt sorry for me. Because why would anyone—especially someone like him—ever like someone like me?

"I hate seeing you like this, Melody," Cece's voice is soft. "But I also know you need time."

"How's she doing?" Declan's voice chimes. I keep my head hidden in the pillow, but his footsteps make their way inside.

A small thud echoes almost like he dropped something into the room—my things probably.

"Has Cass texted you, yet?" she asks instead of answering him.

"No. It keeps going to voicemail like he's trying to call someone."

"I haven't seen anything on Melody's phone."

Because I blocked and deleted his number. I had to before I got the stupid idea to look at his texts or hear him tell me lies—like Jay had.

"Mel, we're going to check with Cass… see if he can tell us anything," Declan says, but I don't respond.

"I don't know what to do," Cece tells him.

"Neither do I… but I know things aren't right. Something's wrong. I can feel it in the depths of my chest."

Cece hums softly, "Then we should get to Cass."

"Do you think she'll be okay here by herself?" he asks. I can feel his gaze even through the blanket.

"I just think she needs a little bit of time to be alone. Besides, Ophelia is next door if anything."

Their words begin to fade as the darkness swallows me whole. Everything around me is gone.

And I'm left with nothing, but the tears in my eyes and a broken heart.

33

GRIPPING MY LUNGS

CASSIUS

I can't find Melody anywhere and it's starting to bring back past memories. Memories I wanted to keep buried for good. But I can't give up. Not until I find her. Not until I know she's safe—that she's alive.

"Where's Declan?" I asked Cece, a little harsher than needed, but the tight feeling in my chest wasn't a good sign.

She shrugged her shoulders, wrapping her arms around herself. "I think he went home or something."

He would have never left without telling us though. He would have at least texted. "But he usually has practice."

"His teammates said he wasn't there."

Now I knew something was wrong.

I waste no time parking the car outside and race into the house. I head straight for Melody's door and try the knob, but it's locked. I knock, "Melody. Moonlight, please open the door."

Nothing. No sounds. Nothing.

"Melody?"

She doesn't answer. I swallow hard. Anxiety crawls up my arm and finds its way under my skin. It carries on, gripping my lungs. I try taking deep breaths, but it's hard. A rope coils around my chest, strangling my heart.

"Melody!" I call out, banging against the door harder. "Melody!" My shoulder hits the wooden barrier. There's no pain as I keep going.

"Declan! Open the door." He didn't answer though. There was no sound. Nothing.

Pain.

Sharp shooting pain spread through my entire chest. I pounded my hand against the door again. "Declan!"

Another sharp pain stabbed through my heart like a needle. It hurt. It hurt so fucking much. My shoulders slammed the door down.

And the pain began to subside... but there was Declan...

My brother's voice is faint in the background, and so is my sister's. Hands grab me and try to pull me away, but I keep at it. I don't stop until the door breaks and I'm inside.

My blood ran cold, but my feet moved quickly to the bedside where Declan lay—an open bottle of pills in his hand.

It's almost like I'm reliving that day. My body shakes, frozen in place. I see him there, on that empty bed, but I know he's not really there.

There's no Declan.

There's no Melody.

No laptop on her desk. No books or papers around. The room is empty and cold.

"She left, Cassius," Cece's voice crawls into my ears.

Because of her father.

Because I wasn't prepared to face him.

Because they didn't tell me.

"Where'd she go?" I turn and look between my siblings. Both not meeting my gaze.

"She didn't say," Cece tells me.

"Bullshit," I spit. "You're her friend. You know everything. Why didn't you tell me about her father?"

My sister flinches, taking a step back. "I-I wanted you to—"

"Suffer right? Almost losing you and Declan, losing Mom and Dad… none of it was enough," I shout.

"I wanted you to be happy!" She cries as her hand clings to the sleeve of my shirt.

"Not everyone can find happiness, Cece." I pry her fingers off of me. "This world isn't shits and giggles. You know that firsthand."

"Cass, chill out." Declan chimes in, stepping between me and Cece.

"I'm so sick of being chill for everyone!" I shove him. "Keeping myself in check, being the support everyone needs from me."

"No one asked you to."

"Who was going to do it, Deck, you? After all the stress and hate throughout the years? As if I'd let you nearly kill yourself again."

"That's not your fault," he admits.

"You did it because of Mom," I tell him. "Because she paid more attention to me and Cece. And then Cece thought she was the problem." Their arms wrap around me, pulling me into them. I want to pull away, want to let all the anger and dark feelings wash me away into the depths of its ocean, but my shoulders shake, my body drops and I cave into their support. Declan's shirt is soaked. I hadn't even noticed I was crying.

But, I don't care. It's all too much. I lost so many people in my life. People I've cared about. And now I've lost her too.

My moonlight.

My guide in the dark.

BUT I'M TRYING

MELODY

I'm dating her out of spite.

It doesn't matter that it's been over a week since I've heard him say those words—they still crush my heart.

I curl into Cece's bed, dragging the blanket over my face, trying to tune out Cass's voice in my head. He's in there, repeating every single line he'd said to my father that day. I can't concentrate on schoolwork or my stories. I'm stuck—glued to this bed and honestly, I kind of just want to crawl under it.

A sudden, rough tug on the blanket spins me in the opposite direction of the wall. I glance up, catching Declan—a face I don't want to see.

Not when he's the spitting image of his brother.

Tears swell in my eyes for the fifth or sixth time today. I'm not even sure anymore. I've lost count since the day I heard his brother talking to my dad. Declan's face blurs, but his presence stays.

The bed dips as he takes a seat on the edge of the bed. His hand wraps around my shoulder, pulling me into his chest and letting me sniffle away. He smells sweet, like cotton candy —as usual.

"Melody, I can't have you spending the week before finals crying."

"I don't care." I try to push, but he keeps a tight hold on me.

"If you're going to be crying then I need you to tell me what the hell happened?" His fingers gently rub up and down my arm. "What did my brother do to make you leave?"

My eyes close tight, keeping the tears from falling even more. "Ask him."

"I did, too many times. Now I'm asking you."

I swallow hard, lifting my head. "He.. told my dad he started dating me to get back at him. He feels sorry for me and doesn't actually like me."

"My brother, Cassius, the guy who's been beating himself up for weeks said that?" he asks. Flecks of green swirl in Declan's eyes—something I'd never seen before.

I nod.

"No," he says, shaking his head. "I don't believe it."

"It's true," my voice comes out in a whisper. I still don't want to believe such words came from Cassius's mouth, but they had.

And I was still bleeding out from his wound.

"Melody." He lifts my chin, forcing me to look up at him. His other hand covers mine and brings it to his chest. "My chest has been feeling hollow ever since you left and it's not me. It's him. Cass is fucking devastated."

Why is he doing this to me? Pieces of my heart chip away as I listen to his words—to the desperation lingering in them. "Now tell me, why do you believe he meant those words?"

Because I don't see how anyone can really love me for me. To not just feel sorry for me. For having short arms, for having a disability. I've lived so long with these limitations that I don't know how to separate myself from them. To know where they end and I begin. How can Cass's words be lies if even I feel sorry for myself? For the situation I'm in—the one I don't want to be in.

I don't want to feel this way, but I do and it's hard.

But I'm trying…

And I shouldn't be down on myself. Shouldn't project my internal issues on Cassius.

He's been nothing but understanding since we've met.

"There's more to this story, Melody." His words catch my attention. "This isn't the ending. You just need to realize it."

"Then what is it, then?" I ask.

The corner of his lip breaks into a smirk—like he was waiting for me to ask. "The third act break-up, Miss I write romance for a living."

A bubble of laughter comes from my chest. I rub my eyes and shake my head. Declan was one of the last people I wanted to see here—but I think he might be one of the best. "Life isn't a romance novel."

"It can be." He shrugs. "If you fight for it."

"Someone sounds like they read a lot of romance."

"Only when Ophelia has a gun to my head." He smirks. "But seriously, Mel. If not for him, do it for me because, this shit," he taps our hands against his chest, "it doesn't feel good."

He lets my hand slip from his and pushes himself off of the bed. "There's also the fact that you're cooped up in my sister's room and I'm sure she wants it the fuck back."

Sweet one minute and something else the next... that's Declan for you.

But, he's right—other than the fact that Cece wants her room back.

I'm the writer of my story.

And I'll make the ending a good one.

35

A LOT LIKE MY CHARACTER

MELODY

*B*e brave, be bold, be ballsy.

The words sink into my brain as I stare up at Inked Hearts. My temporary tattoos faded, just as my depressive state had.

The semester was nearly ending, and I needed to get things situated with Cassius—before we were beyond repair.

We could figure things out... together. And what better place to talk than at Inked Hearts—where we began?

The tall, dark-haired man I've seen once before lifts his head as I step through the doors. He looks at me and pushes his chair back from the front desk. He stands at his full height, about a foot taller than me—around the same height as Cassius. His emerald eyes assess me, dipping down to my arms.

"Melody, right?"

I nod in response, taking in his broad shoulders and arms nearly being suffocated by his shirt. He might as well be a bodyguard...

"I'm Maverick," he says, his voice a bit gruff. He must be the grump of the shop. "One of the other artists in the family."

Family? He looks nothing like Cassius or his siblings. Then again, Julien and I hardly looked alike. Maybe he was a cousin or something.

"Is Cassius in?" I ask, rocking back on my heels.

"Yeah, he's with a *client,*" I can't help but notice the bitter tone in his voice, "but he should be done soon."

He holds his hand out, inviting me to sit, and I do. My fingers fidget in my lap, knee bouncing. Maybe this wasn't the best idea.

"Did you want a tattoo or something?" Maverick asks, grabbing my attention. He rounds the desk and leans against the front of it. His arms cross over his chest, making his arms pop out even more. Unlike Cass and Declan, his tattoos are different. Inked paintings of trees reside on his forearm and mountains are cut off at his sleeve.

I wonder what else he has...

"More trees and mountains," he gruffs out.

My eyes snap to his and heat rushes to my face. "I didn't mean to say it out loud."

He shrugs. "Better to tell you than to have you trying to search for yourself. I can see the curiosity sparkling in your eyes. Or maybe that's inspiration."

Probably the latter because the more I stare at Maverick the more I see it... the more I see a resemblance to my character—to Sergio.

"Both? You look a lot like my character."

He draws his eyebrows together. "Someone you drew?"

I shake my head instantly. "No. I can't draw. I'm not talented like Cassius is. I write books."

"Wait." He leans back against the desk, rubbing his hand

over his chin. "You're not talking about Sergio Accardi from that book online Ophelia and Cece have been trying to get us all to read."

"You're reading it?"

A small curse leaves his lips along with a chuckle. "I'm not, but I read it over Cece's shoulder once. I'm more into poetry."

I would have never guessed.

"Well, Melody, do you want a tattoo or something? A fake one I mean, I know Cass said you couldn't have one before."

"No. I honestly just came here to talk to Cassius. I thought it'd be nice to talk somewhere we wouldn't be disturbed."

"And you couldn't do that at home... where you live with him?"

My shoulders stiffen and my gaze drops to the floor. "I'm not ready to go there yet."

"I get it, trust me." He hums, pushing off the desk. "It's a small shop. Everyone talks—Cece talks."

"Oh." Of course, they did. They were family.

"I'm not one to meddle. That's her job, but mind if I give you a little advice?"

"I have a feeling you're going to give me it anyway."

"Not everything is as it seems. I know if I were to have ever said what he said, I'd follow it up with the truth."

There's more to this story.

That's what Declan said to me when I last saw him... and now Maverick—someone I don't even know is hinting at Cass saying more than just what he said.

Did I walk out before hearing the entire conversation play out? Was this all just a misunderstanding on my part?

"I don't do well with puzzles," I tell him.

"No, but you're a writer. That means you can at least think of different scenarios as to why he'd say that."

"You're not going to just tell me?"

Maverick smirks, shaking his head. "Nah. That'd be too easy. You gotta figure it out by yourself, like all the characters in your books do."

The sound of a door opening catches our attention. My head tilts, looking around Maverick toward the hallway. The beautiful waitress from the diner—his ex walks out of the room—Cass's room.

Ask him out before his ex tries to.

Cass steps out after her, both laughing. She turns to him, placing her hand on his chest.

My heart stops, but I can't look away. It's like a slow-motion movie. She lifts herself onto her toes and inches close to his lips. But before they can even kiss, I turn from all of them and bolt out of there.

I'm too late...

36

I LOVE YOUR DAUGHTER

CASSIUS

The moment Cara leans up, puckering her lips, I take a step back. The sound of Maverick's voice calling out Melody's name catches my attention, and I glance over to the waiting area just as she runs out. *Shit. Shit. No. No. No.*

Cara grabs my hand, keeping me from running after her.

"She already left you." She tilts her head, pouting her lips. "Why not give us another chance?"

"Not going to happen, Cara." I pull my hand from her grasp. "Mave can ring you up."

Without another glance at any of them, I run out the door. Melody got a head start and there are so many places she can go. Campus, her parents, our place. I make out her figure in the distance and head her way.

My feet move on, slapping against the concrete as fast as they can. Rain drips from the sky for two whole seconds before the downpour begins. And honestly, I don't fucking care.

I have to reach her.

Melody might have left first, but I'm faster. My arm reaches out to her elbow and I grab it, spinning her.

Only... It's not her. Shit. "I'm sorry. I thought you were someone else."

Letting go, I take a deep breath and keep going, and going. I search the entire campus, all the public places at least. My apartment, back at the tattoo shop, and then finally, her parents' house.

I bang on the door and it's opened almost immediately by her mother.

"Cassius, what are you doing here?"

"Looking for Melody," I tell her as I catch my breath.

"She hasn't been here." Mrs. Watson tells me, drawing her eyebrows together.

"Melody hasn't been home—our place. We live together. I don't know where else she'd be if she's not here."

"She did say she was staying with a friend. Come inside, I'll give her a call." Melody's mother walks away and I stand there for a while, unsure if I should do as she asked.

"Mr. Valencia," Melody's father draws out my name, but I don't bother to look over at him—I'm too busy waiting for his wife to return. He moves closer to the door, where I'm still standing, and holds out a towel. "Dry yourself off and come inside."

My gaze drifts up to him. Mr. Watson looks almost as bad as I do. Dark circles rest under his eyes. His hair looks like it hasn't been brushed, and his suit... is wrinkled as hell. "You going to tell me to stay away from your daughter or that you're shutting me down—" He holds his hand up, and I stop, letting him speak.

"No, none of that." He drops his hand to the side and sighs. "It's about Melody."

"I haven't seen her," I cut him off before he can continue. "I don't know why, but she just... vanished."

"She did that with Jay as well."

Her ex.

So what? Did she just always skip out on people and not let them talk things out?

No.

No, that isn't fair of me to think. Melody has her reasons. I just wish I knew exactly what they were.

"Despite what you—or anyone else—may think, I want what's best for my daughter."

"So you want to keep her away from me and my siblings because it's best for her?" I ask, raising an eyebrow. I want to be sure I'm hearing exactly what he wants to express.

"Melody is a beautiful soul. She doesn't need to be corrupted by—"

"With all due respect, Mr. Watson," I cut him off for the second time. "What's best for you or what you think is best could be harmful to others. If you don't like Trans people, for whatever reason, then fine, but don't feed your beliefs onto another. Melody is a beautiful person and the fact that she is so accepting of all kinds of people regardless of their gender identity, sexual orientation, or disability reflects that. She deserves to have her own beliefs. Whether they align with yours or not."

Before he can say anything else, Mrs. Watson returns. She moves beside her husband with a smile on her face. Taking the towel from him, she hands it to me and I take it, drying the rain from my face. "Thank you."

"You're welcome." She says, looking me over. "She was very upset with the both of you for the conversation you had on her birthday."

"Melody was listening?"

She nods.

"Fuck, I'm sorry. I didn't mean it... the first part. I love your daughter, Mrs. Watson."

"Viola." She smiles. "And I know. I knew it the moment I saw you. The way you handle her with care and the sparkle in her eyes. You wouldn't be dripping on our porch if you weren't in love with her." She chuckles softly, glancing down.

"My James is the same. He has a terrible view on certain things though." She intertwines her fingers with his. "Life made him that way. However, I do not expect you to forgive him for his words or actions. He has yet to earn anyone's forgiveness and respect."

No. He didn't. And as much as I wanted to ask why she was with him, I wouldn't do that. Not with him standing beside her. It'd be disrespectful.

"Sometimes people like my James need someone to humble them and show them the errors of their ways."

I don't understand, at least not fully, but I really don't think it's my place to, anyway.

"Melody is staying with her friend on Campus. Cece, she said her name was."

My sister. Of course, it's Cece. Normally visit her, make sure she's alright, but I haven't. She's been waiting for me to find Melody curled up in her bed and here I've been mopping and keeping busy instead of being smart.

I hand Viola back the towel with a smile. "Thank you. I promise I'll make things right with your daughter."

"I know you will."

With those final words, I rush back as fast as I can to campus. To my sister's hall.

Be brave, be bold, be ballsy.

Melody's mantra is inked on my skin, soaked into my brain.

Everything racing through my head says I need to make things right. For me. For her. For us. Our future. A future I never thought existed. I never knew someone could have such a deep impact on me until I met Melody. And fuck, if I lost her for good that'd be the end of it.

I don't bother knocking on Cece's door and, instead, use the card key she gave me weeks ago. My gaze lands on Melody's small figure.

My heart stops, my breath slows, and I freeze the moment her moonlight eyes meet mine.

It takes her a minute to shake the sudden shock. A blush creeps up her neck and up to those beautiful round cheeks. Her pouty lips open and my name barely comes from them, but it's enough to snap me out of the hold she has.

"Cassius…What are you doing here?"

"I came to apologize."

WRITERS OF OUR OWN STORY

MELODY

Cassius—the last man I want to see—stands in the doorway. Wet droplets drip from his face. His soaked white t-shirt is practically see-through and clings to his well-defined body. I can make a clear outline of his opened chest tattoo. Heat rushes to my face, coating my cheeks pink—I'm sure.

"Cassius…" His name barely slips through my lips as my gaze drifts up to his sunlight eyes. "What are you doing here?"

"I came to apologize."

My eyebrows furrow. Why would he apologize? He was with his ex. I'd just seen them nearly an hour ago about to kiss.

"You don't need to," I tell him, refusing to let the pain and tears resurface. "I get it. You want to be with your ex. Not someone like me."

"What? No." He shakes his head, keeping his eyes on my face. "She came by for a tattoo. We had some laughs and then she tried to kiss me. I swear that was it."

"Then what are you sorry for?"

"What I said to your father," he sighs. "I was giving him what he wanted to hear, but right after I gave him that, I explained it wasn't true. Melody, you should know I'd never date someone out of spite."

He glances down as his hand reaches out, but he stops as his gaze falls to my clothes.

"You stole my sweater?" he asks, stepping inside and forcing me to take a step back.

"What else were you going to say, Cass?"

"I asked you a question first, Moonlight." His hard gaze snaps back to mine—full of determination.

I can't help, but answer with a simple nod. A smile creeps up the corner of his lips and he does the same—nodding— before his lips part, continuing.

"Melody, I know it's hard for you to trust someone. Especially after what that asshat of an ex did to you." I fight back a smile and he takes another step closer to me. His hands cup my face. His head lowers, forehead touching mine. "I asked you to be mine because I want to be with you. You're smart, beautiful, brave, bold, ballsy, and so much more. I love you, Moonlight. So please, forgive me for making you believe otherwise."

My eyes flood with tears. No one has ever said such sweet words to me. Words I've always wanted to hear. And I believe them I do—at least, I want to. Especially with those sunlight eyes full of love and sincerity.

"I was finally getting over my fear of trusting until I heard what you said to my dad. And then seeing Cara didn't help. I want to forgive you. I want to trust you..." Tears blur my view of him. A small cry bubbles up from my throat. "I'm sorry I know you're not that cruel. I'm sorry for not communicating."

His lips press to mine, stopping me from continuing further. His thumb washes away the tears at the corner of my eyes. "You have nothing to be sorry about, Moonlight. That's on me. I have a lot to make up for and it'll start with getting your trust back."

He presses another quick, sweet kiss to my mouth. "I love you, Moonlight."

I sniffle and scoff as a smile grows on my lips. "I love you too, Sunlight."

"Now tell me I can take you home and tear my sweater to show you just how sorry I am."

Cassius reaches up, wiping another tear away and I can't help but laugh. "Let's go home."

"Finally!" Cece and Declan's voice comes from behind Cassius. He drops his hands from my face and looks back, giving me room to see them as well.

The two are smiling at us. Declan's arm wraps around Cece's shoulder. "I knew my talk with her would give her some inspiration."

"Does this mean you're leaving me?" Cece asks before anyone can respond to Declan.

"Yes, she's leaving you and coming home with me." Cassius reaches for my hand, weaving our fingers together. "Where she belongs."

"What about Inked Hearts?" Declan asks, "I thought her dad threatened he'd tear it down or something if we didn't stay away from her."

I blink twice, looking up at Cassius. Was that true? I couldn't even ask. Cassius looks at me, smiling as if there's nothing to be worried about. But I am. "You can't lose your job because of me. You love it."

"How do you know that?"

"Cassius…"

"Melody." He smirks. "Trust me, it's fine. He can tear it down if he wants. As long as I have you. And besides, the building doesn't make up Inked Hearts. We do. So as long as we're still doing our thing, no one can take that away."

His sunlight eyes shimmer—determined and full of heart. I love this side of him, all sides. I can't wait to see more and grow with him.

To be writers of our own story.

And give ourselves a happy beginning that people will be inspired by.

Mafia Story
Sergio P.

The world didn't end in a bang or a whisper, but rather one scream at a time. I jolt from my bed. The piercing scream in the night is enough to shake my sleepy haze. Outside, feet shuffle. Our men ready. Ready and prepared as I am.

Adrenaline pumps through my veins, but I don't let the excitement or fear get the better of me. Dangerous situations call for a leveled head. And I need to keep it straight in case of anything.

My hand reaches under my pillow, feeling for that cold smooth pistol. My fingers wrap around the grip as I plant my feet on the ground. I'm quick to slide on a pair of shoes and the bullet proof vest beside my bed. Never thought it'd come in handy this way.

But war springs up when we least expect it, especially direct attacks. Warning this time.

Another scream follows. I step closer to the door and past my ear to it. Nothing but footsteps still, luckily. My hand slides over the knob, turning and pulling it open.

Men in suits might down the hall, but one stands by my door. Vincenzo glances over, his arms crossed over his chest as he pushes himself off the wall.

His hard gaze gives me the answers I need. The betrayers finally decided to carry forward instead of hiding behind their fucking facades.

FOREVER INKED

CASSIUS

FIVE MONTHS LATER

"Are you sure you want to let him do this?" Melody asks over the buzzing sound coming from Maverick's tattoo gun. I'm not sure if she's asking me or my cousin, but if there's anyone I trust more than myself to mark my skin with ink, it's Maverick. Sure, Declan knows what he's doing—as does Cece —but Maverick is careful, much like I am. Besides, my siblings would fuck up the tattoo on purpose and I wanted this one to be perfect.

A hefty laugh comes from him and the needle is lifted from my skin. I take the moment to look down at my chest. He's almost done. Little red spots bubble over the first letter, but that's okay. It'll heal in no time.

"Cass is a grown-ass man. If he wants to make stupid decisions, like tattooing your name on his skin, then so be it."

"You'd know a lot about stupid decisions, huh?" I smirk, shifting my gaze to the ceiling—Maverick's ceiling. Painted cracks make it look like the ceiling is open. Hovering above is a tree with green leaves and a blue sky.

After Melody and I got back together, our shop received more clients—and a donation from Redwood U, which I'm sure was thanks to her father. He hasn't been around my siblings or the shop since and I like to think it's his way of supporting us without showing it.

But this ceiling mural was the first thing we added with the extra money. We even got some new tools for the shop—which is great because we needed them.

Life seems to be coming together and I can only be grateful for it all.

What I'm not grateful for is the way Maverick digs the needle into my skin more than needed. I suck in a breath, inhaling the smell of ink that surrounds his station.

"We're talking about you making stupid decisions, not me," he says.

"How is Xylina?" Melody chimes in, fishing for the same trouble.

"She's fine," he grumbles. "Which you'd know if you just texted her instead of asking me."

"But you're her—"

"Keep it up and I'll make sure your boy gets an infection."

I glance over at Maverick. There's no denying the prideful smile on his lips. Despite his empty threats, he's happy. We both managed to do fine. Him, fixing things with his best friend's ex-girlfriend, and me, capturing my Moonlight. "Don't worry, he can't actually do that."

"So, Melody," Maverick pulls her attention away from me. "How's Aria's story coming along?"

"I finished it." Melody beams, smiling with pride.

"So what's next? Are you gonna publish it?"

She shakes her head, lowering her gaze from him. "I have to go through and edit it, rewrite some scenes, and then *maybe* get it to an editor so I can eventually publish it."

"One step at a time then." Maverick chuckles. The buzzing sound dies down and he rubs a cloth over my chest, carefully placing plastic over my new ink. "Just know we're all here to support you. The girls have mentioned wanting a signed copy."

They aren't the only ones. Mr. and Mrs. Monroe have asked as well. Hell, Mr. Monroe went as far as *donating* money so Melody could eventually publish her book and get it out to the world. I just have yet to tell her.

I sit up slowly, reaching for Melody's hand. My gaze catches hers, eying the word etched in my skin. She says her nickname softly with a smile.

"This way I have you everywhere I go," I tell her. My finger toys with the engagement ring I slid on her finger a month ago, when I graduated college.

I'm ready to give her the wedding band—once she finishes her next year. But for now, this is a token so she and everyone else knows, it'll always be her.

"Moonlight," she grins, reading the word again.

My hand squeezes hers gently and I lift her hand to my lips, pressing a small kiss to it.

"Forever inked on my tattooed heart."

THANK YOU!

A huge thanks goes to YOU from the bottom of my heart for picking up this book. Cassius and Melody's story is special to me, so it means everything to me that you took the time to read and follow along. It's because of people like you that make it possible for me to do this author thing.

As always, I have to thank Joey, my partner, for his unconditional support, for always lifting me up when I'm feeling down, for putting my hair up in a ponytail after I have a mental breakdown because I can't put it up neatly, for letting me walk around with a container of animal crackers, and for inspiring scenes I write in these books.

To my mom, my siblings, and everyone in my family who always cared and loved me regardless of my disabilities. Even though you sometimes smothered me, you always made me feel *normal* when you'd tell me to grab things that were too high for me to get.

To my friends who've over the years become a second family to me. Always treating me like an equal and shitting on me every chance you get because that's just what we do.

To Amanda, for letting me *"steal"* her character names,

inspiring me every time we write together, and for being my soulmate because friends can be soulmates too.

To Anna, I literally cannot thank you enough for all that you have done for me. The cover, editing, and most importantly, a great friend. To Kaitlyn, my supporter and friend since those earlier days on Wattpad. To Letty, one of my biggest fans and a great friend who claims all my MMCs as her book boyfriends. To Ashley, the best person to reach out and talk to about stories, characters, and anything else. To my beta readers, you all are my lifesavers. Without you, this book might have not made sense.

ABOUT THE AUTHOR

Darlene Rodriguez is a self-published disabled author who writes romances for the daydreamers.

Her passion for writing grew from a place of loneliness. She always felt different and like she did not belong, so she turned to daydreams which she eventually put to paper. She hopes these stories will give others a place to belong and feel loved.

Want to stay in touch?
Follow me on social media!